42nd bestseller list!

Praise For Different Stuff

"Spellbinding!"   "Compelling!"
"Skillfully crafted!"
"Riveting!"   "Nice pictures."
"Gritty Realism!"
"My brain cells have never felt so rested---."
"Wrenching"
"Captivating"
"Suspenseful!"
"Evocatively drawn"
"Absolutely no thinking required."
"Praiseworthy!"   "Praiseable!"
". . .highly effective, no-nonsense prose. . .well. . .maybe some nonsense"
"A page-turner!"
I couldn't put it down!"
"I couldn't pick it up!"
"Lots of obfuscatory syntax!"
"Hugely satisfying first effort!"
"Sensational imagery!"

Paradoxical!   *Enchanting!*   *Thrilling!*   *Stupid!*

Different Stuff

by

Bill Zaner

Butch & Debbie -
Let's have a s<u>ill</u>y
MOM<u>EN</u>T once
in a while --- pl<u>ease</u>!!!

Bill Zaner
Boerne Texas
1-10-03

Different Stuff
Copyright 2003
Bill Zaner

Cover art and illustrations by him

Bill Zaner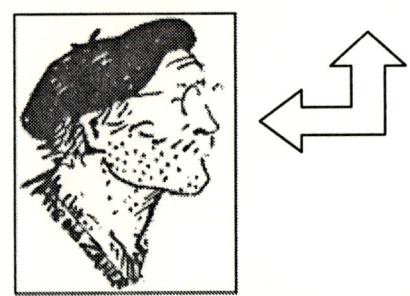

ISBN 1-932196-19-6

A Park Imprint
P.O. Box 1785
Georgetown, TX 78627

Printed in the United States of America

All rights reserved. No part of this book may be reproduced or transmitted in any form by any means, electrical or mechanical, including photography, recording, or by any information or retrieval system without written permission of the author, except for the inclusion of brief quotations in reviews.

*Dedicated to my loyal readers,
all three of them,
who've been only slightly brain-damaged,
I hope, from reading "Different Stuff"
for nearly fifteen years.
I love you all for appreciating a "Silly Moment."*

Table of Contents

Turn Pages — Be Surprised!

Third Theory Explained

Unlike school boards that opt to teach their students one theory or the other – creation or evolution – we here at "Different Stuff Academy" believe in giving our children a complete education.

We will reveal all sides of every question. Our kids will be fully prepared to cheat on college entrance exams and will not go into those tests without every scrap of info that we can provide about meaningful debates.

They need pertinent data about all three sides or theories of the age-old argument concerning the origin of mankind. Yes, three sides!

We here at Different Stuff have devoted several grueling minutes devising our Third Theory, agonizing over it, fine tuning it and organizing it into a presentable format.

We have decided, finally, that our faithful "Stuffers" should be the ultimate adjudicators, searching as we know they will for loopholes.

We have written down, in simple, straight-forward, mostly four-letter words what we consider to be a logical alternative theory, without any facts at all, of course, to those two extant shop-worn theses purporting to explain whence we came – the Theory of Evolution and the Theory of Creationism.

Our Theory, to be called the Theory of DE-Evolution, is

explained thus:

This race of warm blooded beings we fondly, perhaps arrogantly, call "human beings" began, we believe, as much more fully developed entities, both physically and mentally.

When we first appeared on Planet Earth, we were not fat, ugly and stupid. We were physically perfect, beautiful one and all and utterly brilliant too, in that we employed a full 15 to 20 percent of our brain cells in the process of thinking.

We knew world peace. We got along with everybody. We lived in perfection.

Then, ah yes, then. Lots of bad stuff happened, such as computers and golf and cell phones and SUVs. Oh, Lord, the stuff that those and other so-called improvements and conveniences did to us as human beings.

We stopped communing with Nature. We used all our water and labor in keeping the golf place green. We endangered our fellow beings by trying to drive our cars and talk on our cell phones at the same time. We deteriorated into aggressive behavior because we assumed nobody could hurt us in our armored sports utility vehicles.

We didn't have to use our own brains hardly at all. The computers had better, more efficient brains than us, didn't they? And we got lazy and warlike because of all the conveniences available to us. So we went downhill, baby, fast.

Some millennia after we succumbed to living the so-called "good life," we began to de-evolve as a race.

We gradually, over some thousands of years, probably six, de-evolved ourselves into what could be called "lesser beings."

Our place on the evolutionary scale has a smaller number now. We are not Number One anymore. We've slipped.

If we can't recover the mental and physical superiority we started with, according to our Third Theory, we are in danger of de-evolving further yet, even into a level of bottom feeding creatures such as politicians or telemarketers or, even worse, Rush Limbaughs or Jerry Springers.

The Grass Roots Critic: Goofy Stuff

From perusing the "check-out counter" tabloids, one services an entirely unused corner of the cerebellum. One is appalled, amused, abstracted. One is baffled, bemused and bewildered at the plethora, the plenitude of pathological perceptions within the coarse newsprint pages of these parsimonious periodicals!

How has one survived lo! these many decades without the intellectual stimulation provided, if one will but pause at each and every cash register in this great nation of ours?

Take a minute with me, won't you, to scan but a few randomly selected samples of pulp luminosity (and I will provide parenthetical comments):

GIANT BABY DWARFS MOM! (She got a hernia trying to pick him up – he weighs 167 pounds!)

ED MCMAHON CLAIMS TO HAVE JOB-FOUND GUILTY OF PERJURY! (What DOES he do, anyway?)

OPRAH LOSES 436 POUNDS IN THREE DAYS! (But, can she keep it off?)

SOAP STAR SUES SHRINK! SAYS HAIR WILL NO LONGER STAY ON HIS HEAD! (Something is loose, you can bet!)

WORLD'S SMALLEST BABY 4" TALL AND SIX MONTHS OLD, IS WALKING! (But, not very far!)

HEAVENLY VISION OF ELVIS SAVES WOMAN'S LIFE! TOP GOVERNMENT INVESTIGATORS CONFIRM – ELVIS DID NOT DIE! SIGNED HIS OWN DEATH CERTIFICATE! ETCETERA! (I love Elvis stories – they are some of the weirdest of all!)

And, there are loads of "old-age" stories:
94-YEAR OLD WOMAN HASN'T AGED IN 70 YEARS! (Eternal Youth Secret Revealed: she lies like a rug!)

And, vampire tales:
GARLIC BREATH SAVES WOMAN FROM VAMPIRE! (You wouldn't think vampires would be so sensitive, would you?)

Also, monster gags:
MONSTER LIZARD STALKS FLORIDA! (Looking for a monster she-lizard, probably!)

And, of course, no tabloid worth its wood pulp can go to press without – the ALIEN item:
WOMAN RAVAGED BY UGLY SPACE ALIEN! ("Oh, he was horrifying to look at," says the now-recovered woman, a far-away look in her eyes, "but he was so polite."

The advertisements in these publications are not to be missed either, and your critic has not done so. They are so pungent, so rich in folklore and information in their variety of goods and services offered that we will submit for your perusal a separate review in another column, space being the premium consideration it is.

To wrap up, we have but skimmed the surface of the above mentioned troves of literary treasure in the present critique, but we shall delve again and perhaps deeper into their seamy depths. Don't forget, a tree has forfeited its life – can we be so insensitive as to allow that sacrifice to be in vain? I can't resist – just one more!

AMAZING DOG GIRL HAS I.Q. OF 200 – AND TALKS WITH ANIMALS! Wait! One more!

MAN FROZEN IN 1936 REVIVED! (Doctors amazed when man sings two choruses of "Blue Suede Shoes!")

septuagenarianitis

I'm pretty sure all "under sixty-fivers" will not be much interested in today's column. It will seem entirely unrelated to your own existence, therefore, irrelevant.

But, please consider before rejecting: old age shouldn't be denigrated. It's a privilege denied many, as some wise person has said. You, too, might get lucky.

Septuagenarianitis. I myself have just this millennium year acquired this disease. It is an incurable affliction that is treatable, but incurable. For at lease a decade, unless the unthinkable "alternative" occurs.

But so far, at least, in the first 10th of my seventh decade of life, it hasn't been so bad. It's desirable, I think, to actually think about it as little as possible while trying to bear it with some grace and optimism.

I'm treating the whole thing, best as I can, as kind of on-the-job-training, one day at a time, with a relaxed philosophical aplomb. Not too much one can do about it anyway.

You geezers and duffers and codgers will all know what I'm talking about, though. I don't intend to pursue any sort of lengthy discourse on aches and pains, only to congratulate all of us on having the necessary inner strength, determination and perseverance to survive septuagenarianitis.

Courage, too. A steadfastness, a resoluteness. We've all made a pledge, haven't we, to just go ahead and live, to just get on with it.

I see a lot of you doing just that – getting on with it, that is, and it's beautiful to watch.

Heck, I know your joints ache and you take much longer to get rested and it takes a lot less exertion to make you need to get rested.

The ordinary ailments that accompany septuagenarianitis just have to be put up with.

There are some perks, too, that come with it. Let's see, what are they!

Oh, yeah, I remember! (I think I can remember if I can only remember to think!)

We septuagenarians are at that age when we can say almost anything we feel like saying.

We can choose to not hear whatever we don't particularly want to hear, just like when we were teenagers.

We are considered harmless by young people, if aggravating, therefore, we can get away with whatever strange behavior we might choose to indulge in.

And speaking of aggravating, don't you think it's kind of fun to tweak some people and not feel guilty about it? Just to watch their reaction?

I don't know about you, but sometimes being annoying seems just the right thing to do.

What the heck, geezers, we need to balance out the negatives about our condition with just the right attitude of "what you see is what you get, like it or not."

Have we not got more plain horse sense than to continue participating in the rat race? Can't we just sit back and detach ourselves from the constant striving that drives young people?

Yes, we can. And then go take a nap.

odds 'n "Ends 'n "More odds

The return of those ever present black dots:

· Wouldn't it be just about the greatest imaginable testimonial to your life if, as your earthly remains were lowered into the ground, the eulogist would say, with great sincerity, "He was a great man, a certified genius in his field, much beloved by everyone who knew him, a wonderful father and husband and Look! He's moving!"

· If, as the television advertisements have it, four out of five people suffer from psoriasis, does the fifth one enjoy it?

· Why do gorillas have big nostrils? Because they have big fingers.

· We Different Stuffers are still waiting for a president who can properly pronounce "nuclear." Or "Realtor."

· Are there age limits for men wearing earrings? Should a 60 year-old guy go around displaying punctured ear lobes? Or even a 20 year-old guy? Perhaps, in the ever striving for societal gender sameness, we should all get holes punched in our pristine bodies at birth – boys as well as girls – so there wouldn't be a stigma attached to all this body-piercing we're doing. Heck, we guys could proudly display our eyebrow, nose, cheek, lip, tongue and ear holes without checking in with the fashion police each time we decide to desecrate ourselves.

· What I think is that the 60 year-old pierced guy probably has a 26 year-old girlfriend he thinks she thinks his earring is cool. Probably loves his tattoo, too!

· It's about time professional baseball players went out on strike. It's been several years now that these poor guys have been trying to make ends meet on their meager $12 million a year contracts.

Our hearts go out to them. It's getting so difficult to relax comfortably for those five harsh winter months they're forced to endure on the beach at Waikiki. Poor babies.

· How about this for sick? We heard the other day about one of the most popular video games being played by 10 year-old boys, something called "Grand Theft Auto III." (Were there Grand Theft Autos I and II?) The players get extra points for killing women. We cannot even comment on this one.

· Another sports item: we think it's a durn shame there will apparently be no hockey team in San Antonio. We will have to satisfy our love of mayhem by, oh, going to car races or maybe football games. Or- and we should have thought of it before – devising and playing "Grand Theft Auto IV."

There's always rasslin', too, where we can enjoy watching grown (?) men and women bash and pummel each other.

· Finally – whew! – the ratio of bad drivers to good drivers increases daily with aggressiveness behind the wheel being the cause of most auto accidents. Maybe it's the advertising. We're deluged with car ads which tell us and show us we need to drive fast and splash mud on the other guy. Isn't that just wonderful?

Art — Sure Beats Working

"Art does not take kindly to facts, is helpless to grapple with theories and is killed outright by a sermon."
Agnes Repplier, 1891.

It's always struck me as paradoxical to refer to what artists do as "work." In the normal sense of the word, that is.

Coal miners work, farmers work. Guys who put roofs on houses work, as do guys who smooth wet cement.

One of the hardest workers I ever knew was my grandpa who was a cattle rancher back in the old days before ranching was done from a pickup truck.

You can probably think of many occupations which involve actual work – physical effort plus mental strain – but, in all your imaginings, you'd not call what artists do work, would you?

Oh, the art of sculpting does call for occasional heavy lifting and some sweat of the brow. And, even in my field, easel painting, there is some small amount of physical exertion. Stretching and preparing canvases is fairly strenuous, especially here in my elderhood.

I've always told people not to confuse my basic activities with any kind of labor though – anything this much fun can't possibly be thought of as "work."

Okay. So, when you ask me what I'm doing over at my studio, I'll likely tell you I'm painting or drawing or thinking about painting or drawing, which, as the famous philosopher has it, "to think about art is to do art." Which I believe is true.

Even if you are not a painter or sculptor, but you think about doing a painting or sculpture, you are, therefore, actually doing art. What do you think of that?

I'll tell you this too, when somebody thinks enough of and about a piece (work?) of art to part with his or her hard-earned money to purchase it, that person, too, is being artistic. He's connected with the artist for that time of his purchase and the connection is permanent.

People who buy works of art because they connect with the artist's thoughts, simply because they like the art, are thinking parallel thoughts with the artist and, therefore, are doing art.

That may seem like a stretch, but I believe it. The world is unfortunately over-populated with people who never look at art and who, sadly, cannot do art. If they only knew what they're missing.

So, what are we artists if not working people? I guess it's a matter of semantics. The term "work," also refers to a body of material or product, not unlike, I suppose, a bunch of documents produced by a lawyer or accountant. These people would certainly call what they do "work," don't you suppose?

"If it were easy, anybody could do it," as another well-known philosopher once muttered, more to himself than anything, and from which we may conclude two things – artists do not actually work, though they do produce work, and people who think about art at all – to buy it or just to look at it and think somewhat as the artist thought while producing the art – can regard themselves as artists as well.

I like those two conclusions. They make sense – no small thing in this world of nonsense we live in – though I will undoubtedly continue to make the comment I've always made about what I do. I'm a lucky guy, getting away with doing art my entire life – and it sure does beat having to mine coal!

We are as surprised as you that the opening, obscure, but self-explanatory quote may actually have some connection, if vague, with today's column.

Cousin Goober Wakes Up

Heaven knows, we try to give credit where credit's due. Just look at Different Stuff's universal coverage of all world and local events – we certainly try our very best to allocate whatever honors may be due to whomever in whatever field of endeavor that's in the news at a particular moment in historical time.

We also are conscientious in our handing out blame for booblike behaviors.

We employ the good services of a variety of experts in many fields – our own Grass Roots Critic, for example – an intrepid and dogged reporter of all things cultural, from television and movies to music and literature.

We have Mr. Language Guy, an arbiter of our native language, its use and misuse.

And let's not forget our very own Uncle Willie, Aint Harriet and Cousin Goober, thrice removed, three worthy observers of the social scene who on occasion contribute essays on a variety of appropriate subjects – Harley-riding, snuff-dipping and obscure poetry are but a few matters of interest covered in this column by my barely admitted relations.

It seems that to celebrate the New Year, our cousin Goober, three times removed, was somehow awakened, probably by drunken family members, and was stimulated to take up pen and parchment, shake off some brain cobwebs and treat us to a poem which has no title – give it your own, he suggests.

Some things are best forgot, they say, while others, they say not.
But, how does one remember when,
or how or which they ought to file and keep or cast away,
Or when to laugh and when to weep?
Those choices shall forever be,
That way for you, this way for me.

Cousin Goober, thrice, you know, achieved a nearly erect posture and an almost lifelike demeanor as he thumped down his wrinkled parchment on our desk, deigning to pass a comment or two on the deplorable state of the nearly obsolete art of poetry-writing.

"Whass u-u-u-p!" says the Goobster. "Is they not any wordmeisters left? It's a deplorable state. It'd be a real sad, deplorable state if people don't have some obscure doggerel to entertain themselves with. That's one durn good thing about writing poems," continued Goober. "You can look up a bunch of little-known, ambiguous and indefinable words in your handy-dandy Thesaurus, see if you can make 'em rhyme with each other, sort of trying to explain in intellectually dim language a half-baked philosophical concept that maybe six people on the planet give a hoot about, and then only vaguely."

"What?" we asked.

"See," says he. "You can sometimes accomplish the same obfuscation with a sentence or two of regular prose. But, if you can put it in the form of a poem, folks are a lot more impressed. 'What a brainy guy!' they'll say."

Well, Goob, you're missing your naptime. Wouldn't want that to happen. Thanks for dropping by. We'll wake you up next year.

Boerne Needs – Doesn't Need

We are always compiling lists. Lists for almost anything you can think of – the usual grocery lists, things to do lists, Christmas lists, lists of New Year's resolutions, lists of appointments, phone lists, address lists and lists of lists.

Now we've come up with a list of things we think would make Boerne a better place to live.

Isn't it good to know that we are looking out for our little town? Many of our ideas are, of course, not suitable for printing or have been presented – and rejected – in past columns. But we are dauntless – dauntless, I tell you! – and not at all timid about telling things like we see 'em.

Y'all do understand that the following list of Needs and Do Not Needs are the responsibility of Different Stuff and not our beloved editor and staff of the Hill Country Recorder. Indeed, those worthies have many times denied even knowing us, much less admitting they might possibly have seen any validity in previous ramblings.

(The preceding two sentences comprise what's known in the news game as a disclaimer.)

The List:

Need – people crossings across Main Street. We have duck crossings, but no people crossings which means it's safer to be a duck in Boerne.

We've watched people risk life and limb attempting to achieve the other side of Main Street, many times just giving up.

Don't Need – more ducks. Obviously.

Need – once more our plea goes out to the city planning people. Boerne needs a bypass for 18-wheelers, gravel trucks, buses, giant RVs, Suburbans, Excursions. Get 'em off Main Street. Perhaps the need for people crossings would then be unnecessary.

Don't Need – anymore subdivisions obscuring the hills and valleys around Boerne. Which would eliminate the need for any more realtors, wouldn't it?

Need – to finish up the creek walk stuff we used to hear about in years past. Think about it. A developed area all along the Cibolo where, as in San Antonio, people could enjoy the water way. Okay, we realize it's probably a pipe dream, but, who knows. And it would help make Boerne a better place to live.

Don't Need – a super department store, although we can't stop it now. We do not, however, object quite as much to the super home store – it's across the freeway.

Need – to continue to disallow new building downtown. Our three to four block downtown is what gives Boerne its nice, small-town flavor, thank you very much.

Don't Need – Market Days every month, but we'd like to see the Rod Run twice a year.

This is but a partial list of things we believe would help maintain the ambience of our little town. After all, that's why the tourists like to visit – we have ambience.

Boerne, while not that cute little town we moved to 27 years ago, we can still say "so far so good."
January 9, 2002

National IQ Crisis Feared

At Different Stuff, being of close-to-average intelligence, we think, and additionally, of peripherally sound mind, have arrived in our ordinarily circuitous manner at yet another nearly famous and extremely clear-cut observation pertaining to the current condition of the modern society with which we find ourselves coping daily.

As this column's title succinctly advises, there is a National IQ Crisis. Prevalent in our daily existence are myriad signs of the deplorable state of our guiding philosophies.

There is, and has always been in our beloved country, plenty of tolerance for what we can call "divergent thought," such as is provided for in the Constitution.

Variety is what makes the country great, it is said and we believe that. Even when that variety of ideas includes some that seem to be really far out proposals. Such as:

A "gun-owners" resort community being constructed as we write out there on the desert near Las Vegas, Nevada. That's right, an exclusive home and condo subdivision is going in there, but instead of the usual attractions in your better private and gated communities, instead of golf courses, swimming pools and tennis courts, this one will have shooting ranges.

You can, anytime the notion to shoot your gun comes over

you, amble over to the range and fire off a couple pockets full of bullets.

As the Different Stuff observers understand it, for a mere $350,000, you can purchase a home in this classy addition and be granted in the covenant, not only the right to own and publicly display your collection of armaments, but also, it is inherent in your contract, the right – nay, the invitation – to fire your weapons on your premises.

Yet another IQ crisis indicator:

We've noted a veritable proliferation of seemingly innocuous organizations which are, in name at least, aligning themselves with the long-standing and well-respected "Christianity" group.

These are apparently attempts to give credibility and a "softer" image to their enterprises. We are thinking here of a couple of groups which have not been known heretofore for their charitable and humanitarian goals.

One such organization we heard about was called the "Christian Bull Riding Association." It is difficult for us to imagine a kind and charitable way to ride a bull, though we admit, we've not tried it. We think the bull will still be annoyed, no matter the moral persuasion of the varmint of its back.

Another of the paradoxical situations, if such term can be applied and we think it can, would be one of the longest standing and best publicized of the Christian associated groups in America – the "Christian Wrestling Federation."

Again, we fail to see the difference. This bunch of oversized, over-decorated men are still devoted to crushing the life out of each other in most violent ways – not a very Christian thing to do, in our mind.

Does anybody really buy the concept? Perhaps we are being unnecessarily harsh here, but as our researchers continue to report on interactive social philosophies guiding our communities today, we can definitely detect a diminution in national IQ numbers and feel such is news and must be reported.

Disneyland or Big Bend

I've been visiting my favorite place in the whole world the last eight days, doing my thing, which you may know, is gathering sketches and other information firsthand so I can make some decent paintings – of the Big Bend area of Texas, or wherever else appeals at the moment.

I was thinking real early one morning as I watched the stars rise up from the eastern horizon that I have rather unusual priorities in life.

"I'm sure that's the planet Venus," I muttered, "it has a kind of greenish tinge to it. And look how bright it is. You can actually see the glow before it appears on top of that distant mountain."

I continued the discussion with myself. "When it gets exactly 11 inches above the horizon, the sun will appear in the same path!" And so on went the observations and mutterings.

The very last tiny sliver of moon, perhaps one-16th, was also in the picture for the first few days of my astronomical surveillance – first preceding Venus, almost directly above, then, over the following days, moving a little to the north and finally rising only a few minutes before the sun.

So there, the last morning I watched, was in the pale orangey-yellow glow of late dawn pre-sunrise the tiniest sliver of silver moon, lit directly from below – it would have held water- and above and to the south a bit, the even more brightly shining planet

Venus.

Then a few minutes later, the outlines of the Chisos Mountains would take shape in that wonderful blue-grey of first light.

Another day begins and I thank whatever Supreme Power who's in control of such phenomena for letting me be there to see it.

Well, you're right. It's not Disneyland. I don't even know why I'm not interested in going to Disneyland.

I'm just flat missing out on Real Life, I guess. Everybody wants to go to Disneyland, don't they? Says so right there on TV.

"What are you going to do now that you've captured the pennant?" the talking head asks the baseball star.

"I'm going to Disneyland," he states unequivocally.

"And you?" The head asks the World Champion figure skater or the most recent dot.com millionaire or the recently arrived foreign celebrity.

"We're going to Disneyland!" they enthusiastically answer.

Okay, call me simple.

I'm simple. You're right. I'm not even any kind of expert on the scientific aspects of nature.

What I am is familiar with things natural – stars, mountains, cacti – because I've been hanging out where those things are almost my entire life.

I'm interested in watching the stars rise and the sky and mountains take up their daily chores because I do like to make pictures of them doing their thing.

It's my thing. Also, I'm kind of simple.

Life - not dotcom

Try to get this on your computer:

The thunder rolls across the miles, maybe beginning at the far distant Sierra del Carmen in Mexico. There is a stirring of fresh wind accompanying the bass drum roll.

You can smell it, the oncoming rain, preceded by these little miracles – the thunder, the wind, the cinnamon-like scent of wet creosote bushes, the pure ozone crackling in the air.

In just a moment, individual drops of rain begin to spatter the dust at your feet, each drop creating a tiny splat of sound and a puff of dust from its miniature crater.

Soon, there are too many splats and puffs to count one at a time, and the raindrops become a whooshing torrent, huge drops now slamming into the ground, crackling booms of thunder encouraging the flood.

It is dusk on the desert, and the flashes of lightning are very close, ear-shattering. The sky is ominously black in front of the moving cloudburst. Mammoth clouds are pushed by the wind – fat, bulging clouds ready to rupture and dump their loads of moisture. The low sun spotlights a cloud, tinting it orangey-pink, making the cascading rain look like a solid, red waterfall.

The sounds of the storm are furious, cacophonous, fascinating and frightening. Along with the unearthly sundown colors and the wonderful clean smelling wind, the storm across the desert is an experience, a real life experience.

Maybe one could log on and search, or whatever one does to acquire information from one's computer word/something. something else.com, or org or whatever–and get some information about thunderstorms. There is no doubt a world of facts about them – the how, the why, the where, total and complete explanations which would include absolutely everything about cloudbursts you would ever want to know and them some. Heck, you could impress your friends with your knowledge. Send 'em an e-mail.

Well, okay, one could do that.

But, out there somewhere beyond your desk, out your window where actual nature is, there's a real life experience to be had.

I, myself, continue to work on completing my desert rain experience. As a nature-lover slash artist, I've committed myself to reproducing as near as I can all those sensory perceptions. I'll paint what I can on canvas and write what I can on paper. I've not solved the creosote smell thing – scratch and sniff? Hmmmmm. A new art form?

For now, I can hope to paint and write sensitively enough and will hope you will glance away from your computer open-mindedly enough that some of my real life experience will rub off on you. At least enough to hold you till you can get out there personally.

A Desert Boomer

Hints on Writing Right

Different Stuff aficionados, it's time once again for your semi-every-so often tips on how to write stuff. DS staff realizes how difficult it is for you "regular" people out there to put together a concise, coherent-sounding sentence, where as we semi-professional journalism types regularly turn out these sentences and paragraphs which seem to make sense, and which sound official and correct if you are somewhat distracted by screaming kids or a blasting boombox while you are reading them.

(Editor's Note: He occasionally rambles.)

You see, you must "target your audience" when you write stuff. An example of audience targeting would be when you peck out a one or two word e-mail to a person you know is not devoting more than one or two brain cells to the computer screen – one brain cell per word, you see?

If, on the other hand, you are composing a work of literature which you know will be read by a committee of humorless PhDs on some eastern college campus, then you'd better have all your Ps and Qs in good order. Your ducks better be in a row, too.

If you assume your audience has gone beyond sixth grade reading class, you'll really have to sound basically intelligent, or at least well-read.

We DS'ers believe in writing sort of like the way we think and talk, obtuse as that sometimes may be. When we have a thought, we try our best to record it on our trusty note pad before we forget it and in just the language we'd use were we thinking out loud – which we apparently do a lot, according to our Far Better Half.

Since we are neither intellectual, nor even especially well-read, two states of being, we believe, which will produce gigantic headaches and levels of stress we intend merely to convey to you gentle readers in our weekly epistle whatever of our passing thoughts can be reprinted on this page without arousing the ire of the general citizenry of our fair little city – at least not too much.

(Editor's Note: He occasionally mentally rambles.)

Here are a few rules we'd advise you to follow when you write stuff:

(1) Write about stuff you personally know about – things that have actually happened to you. In case nothing has ever happened to you, move on to number 2.

(2) Make up stuff that could never have possibly happened to you or anybody else you know, but which you think would make a good story.

(3) Take something somebody else has already written, like a saying or a witticism or a cliché and try to put it in different words, change it all around to see if it'll sound better put another way. As, when you say something to somebody and they'll preface their response with "in other words. . ." Doesn't that gripe you to death? If you'd wanted to use "other words," you'd have used other words!

Or, after you've made your statement, somebody'll say, "so, what you're trying to say is. . ."

(4) Our best Different Stuff writing hint, though, is 90 percent of the time just keep it to yourself, ever mindful of the saying, "One's reputation is always enhanced when one keeps silent."

PS Hint: Know the significance of punctuation – slow down when you encounter a comma, pause a bit at a semi-colon, stop altogether at a period, and, most importantly, look up the word "syntax" and call us with the definition, please.

Oddities of Texas Travel – Panhandle

If you are thinking of traveling to Colorado this or any other summer – are you out of your mind? Do you realize what lies between here and there? – read this column before you even pack your bag and start your car.

Note: only wusses fly to Colorado; real tough Texans drive, all the way!

I advise reading this because herein are contained several helpful hints on how to keep from being bored out of your skull by those seemingly endless, uninteresting, colorless miles of flatness and drabness.

West Texas, in general, to casual observers who are not in the habit of noticing stuff, is a very tedious part of the world and you just cannot wait to get through it, to at least New Mexico where you're sure it'll improve.

And it does to a certain extent in that there are some distant blue mountains breaking the horizon.

However, it's difficult to actually look at them for struggling to hold your vehicle on the narrow, bumpy, shoulderless highways so prevalent there in the "Land of Enchantment."

Hint No. 1: There are two kinds of cotton to look at – low cotton and high cotton. (Yes, you will finally be in high cotton.)

Hint No. 2: These fields of cotton are planted in two different ways. There are (A) square-shaped fields and (B) round-shaped fields.

Hint No.3: There are big fields (square and round) of sorghum, both low and high.

Hint No. 4: The corn is as high as an el-e-phant's eye. (Hey, that might make a song!)

Hint No. 5: Count the oil well pump jacks nodding up and down, up and down, as they break the perfect symmetry of the cotton, sorghum or corn fields.

Associated with this, notice the elegant brick homes on the outskirts of most Panhandle towns with their attendant golf courses, Wal-Marts and banks.

Apparently not all farmers are struggling – certainly not those whose cows have to walk around a pump jack to get to the grain bin.

Hint No 6: To avoid being bored by driving across West Texas, the High Plains and the Panhandle, notice, please notice, and enjoy, please enjoy, the wonderful, wonderful place names you'll find as you traverse the vast vastness of the western part of our great state!

Just pronouncing the names of these little towns and settlements will tickle you and help keep you from boredom as you slog away at the curveless miles of unimpeded highway of the Llano Estacado, the High Plains or the Land West of the Pecos.

Look at those green information signs, like the one that says, "Bootleg, Pop. 43." Or Lazbuddie 4 miles." And what an appropriate juxtaposition is "Sundown, Texas" and "Dawn, Texas," practically within hollering distance of each other, as well as "Earth, Texas." All very appropriate, don't you think.

As appropriate, we find, are the towns of "Levelland" (pretty flat country around there!) and Brownfield (the dirt in the area is a kind of reddish-brown color.)

Some of these West Texas towns are famous, too, as the

birthplaces of some well-known Texas entertainment figures. Littlefield gave us Waylon Jennings, for example, and Quitaque (pronounce it Kit-a-Kway) is on the map as the birthplace of the very well-known Bob Wills of Texas Playboy fame. (Turkey, Texas, claims him, too, I think.)

There are others, of course, too numerous to mention, but for sheer fun, my favorites, guaranteed to alleviate your driving boredom, are Wink, Iraan (say Ira-Ann), Spade, Loop, and PaDah.

But the top two funny place names in West Texas must be: Notrees (west of Midland, nearest tree 150 miles east or west). Needmore, just west of Circle Back, home of the "Needmore Gin." Read that sign without giggling!

cloning for fun and profit

After giving the idea my full and undivided attention, using all the neuron power I could muster, literally straining my poor brain, for, oh, 46 seconds, I am able to state, unequivocally, I like the idea of cloning.

There is something so anti-everything – we've ever been taught about it. It's amusing to examine the various ramifications attendant to such pesky scientific experiments in genetic engineering.

Decide what your very best characteristics are, extract those little DNA strings of cells from your body, squirt 'em into one of Mr. Petrie's dishes, add some magic stuff, put everything into a blender, bake the mixture at 375 degrees F. for 45 minutes and viola! Out comes a little bitty exact copy of you.

Just think. You'd be able to guide, direct and mold this small piece of clay into an even more perfect version of you. Exciting, isn't it?

Consider that perhaps a minor adjustment here and there would achieve an actual perfect version of you. I'll tell you, it boggles and bemuses, doesn't it? All those infinite possibilities. .

Okay, so you think we should discuss the philosophical,

theological and psychological ramifications of this cloning business.

Theologically – philosophically, too – the idea of having total control over the physical and mental attributes of one's progeny is appealing, don't you think? Lord knows, the way things are now we bust our buns trying to mold our own particular pieces of clay with, at best, mixed results.

We parents suffer from "parental stress" from sometimes less than successful kid raising. Not a problem with cloning.

Which means, psychologically, having that much control over the outcome of your parental efforts would definitely ease your mind, wouldn't it?

No more stress – what a deal! Just relax and watch yourself develop into another fine human being such as yourself. You've got to like it!

The last time those pesky biologists went and built a large animal, a sheep, my cousin Goober came awake just long enough to pen some appropriate doggerel, that verse titled simply

Cloning:

When Dolly the Sheep feels alive,
It's a state of being for which to strive.
The science of cloning I'd like to borrow.
Then I could be here today – here tomorrow!

We have brushed the cobwebs off Cousin Goober (thrice removed), partially revived him and he has produced another limerick, titling it, again appropriately enough:

Son of Cloning

The science of cloning is back,
The Aggies are giving it a whack.
They've made a new bull, though really we're full.
Of bull stuff we've got a big stack.

We think Cousin Goober (thrice removed) looks almost life-like in this recent portrait.

Little Known "ologies" Baffle scientists

It appears my crack staff of scientific researchers has once again come up with some amazing information – this time about some unusual, and unlikely, new fields of scientific study. These new areas of study could be important new ways for thousands of eager young people to avoid getting actual jobs, believes my crack staff.

We know the "ology" fields are already overcrowded – sociology and psychology especially need to be expanded to accommodate the hordes of new graduates looking for jobs that pay extremely well right off the bat and that allow them to wear nice suits.

You ask, "What are these new "ologies?" Well we're about to tell you.

Mutilationology – being a much needed field of study to benefit those of us outside the scientific community who are perpetually mystified by people's poking holes in their bodies – ears, noses, tongues, eyebrows and other unmentionable parts – in order to display their jewelry.

Or those who have disfiguring ink pictures painfully and permanently engraved on their skins for Lord knows what reasons.

A trained mutilationologist would be able to enlighten us on these prickly subjects.

Apologology – which is the study of, as well as diagnosis and treatment of, people who constantly excuse themselves. "I'm sorry?" "Sorry 'bout that?" "S-cuse me?" An apologologist (bruises the tongue doesn't it?) could treat these poor folks for putting those question marks in there.

Jobology – a new area of scientific study which attempts to explain the general dissatisfaction with employment, supervisors, the workplace, retirement, salary – everything, in fact, about means of making a living. All people seem to care about during their working life is getting it over with, retiring. They can't wait.

There should be a related "ology," crack staff thinks, to cover this total devotion to retirement. Maybe call it "Golfology."

Repeatology – this scientific area specifically covers habitual over-stating and over-explaining by over-educated people who have an over-abundance of facts at hand and an over-abundant supply of words to use in their explanations.

Repetition for the sake of hearing their own voices will be treated by repeatologists. Especially powerful drugs will be injected into speakers the minute they take a breath to say "in other words."

Intentionology. A much-needed field of study, this area of expertise will research and thoroughly examine "intentions."

All people have intentions, as we know. We all "intend" to do a certain thing, "we had it in mind." An intentionologist will issue documentation resulting from various blind tests, placebo tests and general bull sessions, that will prove not all people's intentions are "good."

Please understand, dear reader, that the intentions of my crack research staff are really good ones, not intended to harm, because they like their jobs, though retirement is looking better and better because they'll have more time to visit the tattoo artist who does piercing on the side.

Sorry 'bout that.

In other words . .

Resolutions we forgot

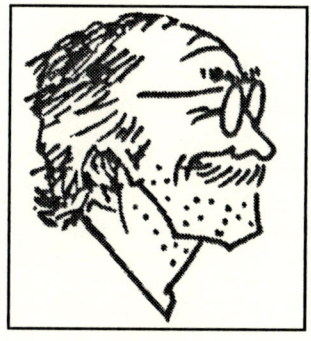

It's hard to believe the Different Stuff staff would actually forget something, but we did leave out a couple of important New Year's resolutions we intended to make – if not actually keep.

As you probably know, "easier made then kept" is the motto the most of us end up ascribing to. All good intentions aside, we tend to fall back into our habitual patterns of behavior, don't we? Our excuse for the most part seems to be, "I'm only human."

All that being said, and I'm sorry to be so obvious, here listed are a few more New Year's resolutions we had every intention of announcing, some perhaps easier than others to stick to:

1. We refuse to hump over the computer pecking out silly jokes to e-mail to our friends. (Easy.)

2. We will not purchase a Cadillac pickup. (Real Easy.)

3. One that bears repeating – we won't buy Bill Clinton's book. (Another real easy one to keep.) (Or Hillary's, either.)

4. When Mizzee and I go on a cruise next month, we will refuse to wear matching "tourist outfits." You've seen 'em – huge khaki shorts so your pipe-stem legs make you look like a donut with toothpicks sticking out of it, along with matching resort-logo T-shirts and white deck shoes with knee-high socks, all topped off with floppy-brimmed sun hats with little badges and pins stuck all

over. No way.

5. We resolve that 2002 will make our 60th year of making and keeping our easiest promise. Once again we resolve not to take up golf. (We've never had any trouble with this one.)

6. In a slightly more serious vein, we firmly resolve not to take politics so seriously that it hurts our relationships with our friends. We have learned over the years that paying too close attention to political demagoguery actually causes short-circuits in our brains.

7. Most everybody we come in contact with over the next year will be glad about our next well-intentioned resolution: we promise not discuss our various and sundry physical ailments with just anybody so that folks have to consider whether they really want to ask us how we are. (We hope this one gets done. We all know better than to inquire after some people's health because they're liable to tell you.)

8. As a final resolution for the upcoming year, we will do our very best to associate intimately only with people who display a sense of irony and humor about this small, funny life we're living.

We can no longer tolerate people who take themselves so seriously that they cannot have any fun and who seem to make sure no one else has any fun either.

(This one will not be easy, we fear. We are too easily fooled about people, despite our claim to be exceptionally observant and sensitive to the human condition.)
No, we make no claim to be able to fix the humor shortage, but we hope to get lucky!

choices

Here in the good ol' US of A we have uncounted opportunities to make choices, a dozen times a day, a hundred times a week, a thousand times a year.

Good choices, bad choices, ones which seem to make no difference at all in the larger scheme of our lives. Silly choices, and stupid ones, too.

We're guaranteed the right to decide for ourselves by the Bill of Rights. (Ever read it? Good stuff.)

Scene One: You're a kid and you're offered drugs by somebody.

Choices:

Take the drugs.

Scream and holler to a teacher or parent that there's a drug pusher in school.

Scene Two: You're still a kid and you have a chance to break into a house.

Choice 1. You go along. What the heck, everybody does it, like drugs.

Choice 2. You ask the would-be burglar, "What are you, nuts? Leave me out of this!"

Scene Three: Again, as a kid, you keep hearing that the way to get ahead and have a good life is to knuckle down and stay in school and study.

Choice 1. You choose to blow it off – you're having too much fun and you and your friends know how uncool school is.

Choice 2. You take a look at the adults who've got a good life, stay in school, study hard and get some new friends.

Scene Four: You're out of high school and are just hanging around waiting for something to happen. Choices you can make:

Keep on keeping on, working a little here, a little there, bumming off your family, getting nowhere.

Get a job, any job, keep it, don't worry about keeping up with your friends, get back in school. (Oh, yes, you'll get a different set of friends with this choice – friends with goals, like yourself.)

Scene Five: You're a young adult now, educated, ambitious, and you're offered two jobs – one pays really well, but you know you'll hate the work, the other pays less, but you love the work.

Choices:

Take job one and tough it out till you're 65, hating your life all the way, then retire and play golf.

Take job two, work at what you love to do, and your whole life will be like retirement.

Scene Six: You're now a parent, and your kid is asking a lot of questions about drugs and alcohol. You choose to:

Tell him to go ask Mom. (Or Dad.)

Give the best answers you can, maybe recalling what you yourself did; go ask the experts with the kid if you don't know the answers.

Scene Seven: Your kid is now a teenager, and it looks like he's making some bad choices. You choose to:

Look the other way and hope for the best.
Confront him about it, tell him his choices are bad, inform him of better options.

Final Scene: AARP has been bugging you to join up, you're getting a few "senior" discounts here and there, you see your grandkids a couple times a year, and you have a lot of time to ruminate. Do you still have choices? Sure, you do:

Move to Florida and play golf.

Stay where you are, play golf, hope your kids move you into a nice nursing home.

Get a motor home and drive to Alaska. Stay there a year and share that state's oil wealth.

Drive your motor home to Las Vegas, sell it, gamble away all the cash in the casinos and on the golf course (you don't play very well), then go move in with your kids.

Choose none of the above, live to 104 and drive everybody crazy.

It's great to be an American and have choices, isn't it?

The Stud Muffin Dove

If this bird were human, he would:
Wear tank tops so you could see his tattoos
Wear his baseball cap backwards
Shave his head and wear a goatee beard
Fill the bed of his pickup with beer cans.
And, his name – his name would be Arnold Schwarzendove. Or, maybe, Clint Eastdove.

He's bad folks, BAD. He hangs out on the top of the rock wall that borders our backyard, up there where we keep the platters of birdseed.

Our intention, in the beginning, was to provide a sanctuary for whatever wild birds were living in our live oaks to have food and water available, and to bird watch.

And it was all proceeding nicely – we could sit in our kitchen and watch all the goings and comings of the cute little birds, watch them peck at the seeds we put there for them, watch them drink and bathe in the birdbath beside the wall.

The bluejays, we think, are especially cute. In spite of their raucous cries, they are fun to watch – the way they take their baths, especially. They'll wade into the birdbath up to their little knees, then dip their heads and bodies into the water, fluttering their wings so their underarms will get wet, then hop to a nearby tree limb to dry off, ruffling their feathers and wiping their beaks on their perch.

The tiny little chickadees are sweet too, as well as the cardinals, finches and titmouses.

We've gotten to observe woodpeckers, sparrows, mourning doves, and just the other day, a pair of Mexican jays who were several hundred miles east of their natural habitat, favored us with a visit, partaking of our spread of food and water, displaying their pretty blue feathers for us in return.

All pretty sweet stuff, right?

Until..The Hulk swaggers onto the scene. Yes, Ol'Arnold Schwarzendove. The Enforcer. The Stud Muffin. Flexing his trapezius muscles and showing his bicuspids.

One wonders how ol'Bluto stays in such good shape since he doesn't have time to eat. He's way too busy fending off intruders – other feathered creatures who have the audacity to try to peck up a few measly seeds for themselves.

Even his own kind, other white wings, are chased, pecked and scolded when they land anywhere near a food dish.

We tried separating the seed platters, thinking Mr. Schwarzendove could be in only one place at a time. Wrong! It tires him somewhat, but, he can still cover the territory.

There is one brand of little bitty bird, a Carolina Chickadee, a little fella about three inches long, who has gotten on to a strategy for successfully getting a seed or two before being threatened by the Big Dude.

He gets his cute little mate to help him, see, and they'll spread their forces, each one going to a separate plate, fluttering off when they're rushed, while the mate grabs a few seeds. Then they reverse the process.

You can see the frustration building in Arnold's little red eyes. We expect him to take up drinking the hard stuff anytime now.

Fall is Falling

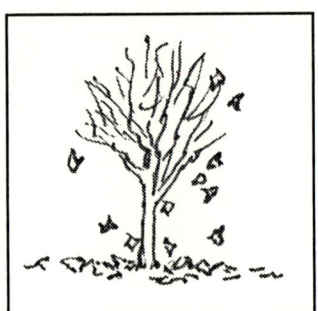

Yes, it is. Out by the highways and byways of the Hill Country there are signs that the season is changing.

There are slight, but noticeable tinges of yellow and red here and there in the trees and grass. The very air feels different – better. You can drive with your window down.

Yes, fall is definitely falling and about time, wouldn't you say? Did it seem to you that this last summer lasted about a year, that it just wasn't going to end? Hot, it was, and dry, and it went on forever.

Never mind what those TV weatherpersons kept saying in their patronizing, overly dramatic broadcasting-school voices. It was a miserable, interminable summer, which just wouldn't quit!

But then that blessed blast of air from the Arctic – the Eskimo wind – was that the most welcome visitor from the north we've had all year? It turned our air from hot and muggy – though never as hot and muggy as Big City air you know! – to "just right" air.

That air felt soft and caressing on my skin. It smelled fragrant. My bare face and arms gave me a temperature reading of a nearly perfect 75 degrees.

It was one of those days when it felt wonderful to turn your face up to the sun and just "bask."

I had driven my pickup to a place I know, maybe one of the last remaining Hill Country hideaways – a place unvisited by masses of people, unknown to all but a few of us "locals."

Heaven help us all if they find (discover) it – it's so quiet there, so pristine and I love being there. In this place, I can really "be."

I listened to myself be alive – heart pumping, blood rushing back and forth, ears slightly ringing with blessed silence.

Here I can ruminate and cogitate, deliberate and formulate. Get a little personal brain exercise, not having to cope with the ruckus of modern daily existence – can't call it life.

I sat in my little close-to-the-ground chair, stirred some color together on my palette and spread it on the paper in my lap. The beginning tinges of yellows and reds and oranges in the foliage inspired me, as always, after the long, hot summer looking at all the brownish greens.

The colors and lines, the golden lights and shadows and the overall look of the scene before me were very pretty. I had to draw lines and make colors. The look and feel of autumn do indeed encourage a painter of landscapes to paint . . .

Is it called "fall" because the leaves fall off the trees? Or is that too obvious an explanation? Anybody know?

Winter, spring, summer, fall. Autumn is a pretty word, "falls" off the tongue pleasantly. Things "spring up" in spring, "sum up" in summer? Oh well, perhaps some more cogitation is called for.

My minimal scratchings and colorings in my sketchbooks may never be judged great works of art or even good works of art by the exalted arbiters of such endeavors – who knows?

The few hours spent that beautiful day doing them, however, must be awarded a prize for well-spent time and I'm grateful to be allowed to do it.

God willing, I'll go back soon.

Just Wondering

All over our crazy planet, crazy folks are doing crazy things. Pretty obvious statement, right? But that's one of the crazy things crazy folks are doing – going around stating the obvious.

Some of the goofier things people are doing on a more or less constant basis are what we're talking about this week, with the ubiquitous Different Stuff Dot preceding each item:

· There is no dearth of craziness over there in the Middle East, we've noticed, and this observation has caused us to wonder. Where do all those bullets go that those folks are forever shooting up into the air? Is their law of gravity different from ours? Has it been repealed? It is unenforceable?

Somewhere, sometime, there will be a veritable deluge, a downpour, a frog-strangler of bullets falling from the sky, assuming, of course, the law of gravity works over there the same as it does here. There you are, standing innocently around, when these little pieces of lead start slamming into the ground. Look out! Gravity works.

· What is it about the beautiful states of Idaho and Montana – maybe Wyoming, too – that seems to attract so many people of the paranoid persuasion who want to live – or hide out – there? Good climate? Low population density? No speed limit?

It can't be because they think they can be anonymous – they

always stick out like sore thumbs. We wonder, even though we know there are fruits and nuts living in other places, especially on the left-hand edge of the country.

· Ever wonder why there are more professional speakers than there are professional listeners? Different Stuff's argument recommends there be more listeners to restore the balance. As it is now, the talkers far outnumber the listeners. In fact, we find a paucity of people with ears willing to use them, to hear us out, to let us have our say, to acknowledge our wisdom.

Perhaps when our babies are beginning to speak, we should take steps to discourage that and other steps to encourage listening – say, teach half (or less) to talk and half (or more) to listen.

· Speaking of youth, ever wonder why if it's so great, why it doesn't last longer? Every day, we geezers wonder about that one. Good hair, smooth skin, endless energy – it just doesn't sustain, does it, no matter how we try to maintain.

That's enough about that subject. Next thing you know, we'll be wondering "what's it all about?"

· Do you wonder why people can't seem to figure out that those old codgers at your high school reunion are you? Why do so many continue to harbor the illusion that time and experience don't change people?

We don't believe human beings are fully developed at 12 or 18 or whatever the current research indicates. In fact, we hold that human beings never achieve complete maturity, but if they do, the turn-around begins so rapidly that there is but an instant of that achievement. Too little notice. Certainly not the well-known 15 minutes of fame.

· Finally, we always wonder if anybody out there is listening. Is our talking falling on deaf ears or are the words of us speakers being absorbed like so many raindrops in a downpour?

We know these are rhetorical questions, but we felt like asking, anyway.

The Fochedo Mega SUV

Once again, we've scooped all the other automotive columns with the news of the soon-to-be-unveiled Ultimate Sports Utility Vehicle, the Fochedo. It is to be a combined manufacturing effort of the big 3 automakers, FOrd, CHEvrolet, DOdge.

In their continuing, highly successful efforts to bilk the American public, the big 3 – SUV makers all – have joined forces to introduce this extremely high-tech, offensively oriented vehicle for use by housewives, teenage girls and guys who just like to drive a "macho machine."

The manufacturer's representatives we interviewed projected astronomical sales figures and, as is usual with SUVs, obscene profits.

Their long-range plan is to invest these monumental profits to start a whole new universe for themselves, complete with a parallel solar system inhabited by – no surprise – gullible citizens with lots more money than sense.

"We'll do very well," the spokesman said.

"Negotiations are underway, as we speak, for the purchase of the nebula star system Cassiopaea. We're cloning SUV owners for immediate colonization of its Earth-like planets."

We had a chance to test drive the new Fochedo and here's our review, as well as a few of the outstanding features standard on the Mega SUV, or "Mad Max" as we've nicknamed it.

Our test drive was fulfilling, exciting, hair-raising. We felt on top of the world as we tooled to the grocery store, putting fear into the hearts of other, lesser drivers.

Of course, the Max is 10 feet high and extremely macho. The

vehicle fairly screams "Don't get in my way!"

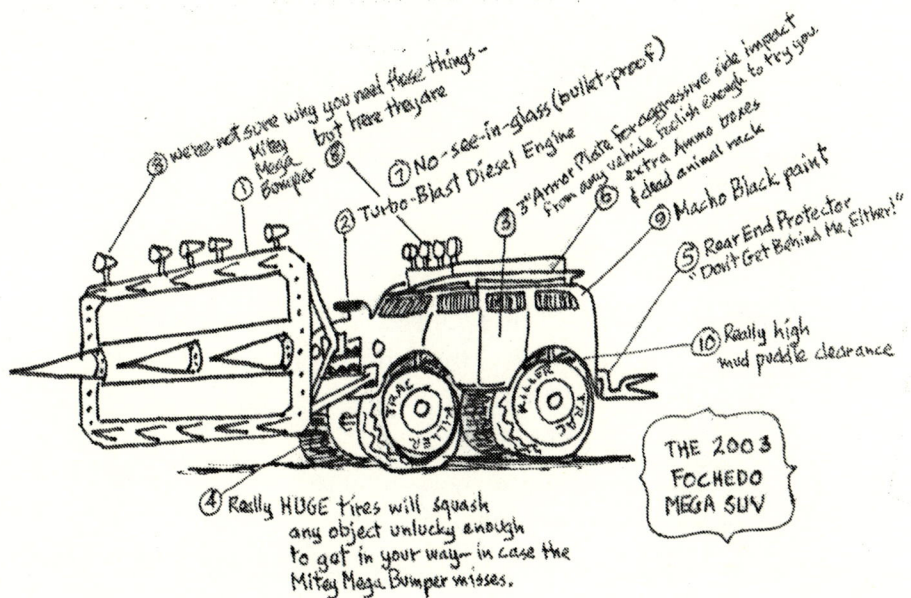

Our recommended rating – 4.5 stars. Five stars could be achieved with the additional option of an extremely loud 18-wheeler air horn —just in case you'd like to celebrate your winning duel with that Winnebago.

In any case, 4.5 is a lot of stars and the Max is getting mighty close to the maker's claim that it is the Ultimate SUV. We love it! This behemoth rules!

The "Don't Do" List

Everyday of hobbling along this tortuous trail of life causes me to think of more and more things that I probably:

Won't get around to doing.

Shouldn't even think about doing.

Might have done when I was a whole lot younger.

Have seen other people do and wished I had the guts to do.

Am content to go ahead and let those crazy fools do.

Am way too smart even to consider.

For instance – and this is not a stretch for me to resist doing – I will not parachute off the Tower of the Americas. Bet the farm on it.

I, along with a lot of other Barcalounger athletes, were aghast as we watched on TV that intrepid, if brain-cell-deficient, yahoo leap off that 500-foot high platform and float down directly into the waiting arms of the law.

"What a nutcase!" we exclaimed. "What did he do that for? The ever-elusive 15 minutes of fame?" Suppose so.

Next on my Don't Do list – I won't make a foolish and disgusting display of myself on any of those so-called "reality" TV shows so pervasively rotting our brains these days. Even if they ask me to, which they haven't.

The definition of "reality" is in question here. I have never even witnessed any of those sick stunts those people seem happy to do. You say they're getting paid big bucks and I ask what price 15 minutes? My world is just entirely too mundane, I suppose.

Next is something I won't do in this life for the many reasons I've enumerated in the past. You guessed it – golf. I just can't bring myself even to imagine participating in such a silly activity where everybody takes the game and themselves so seriously.

But, even considering the serio-comic aspect of golf, I possibly would engage in it occasionally but for the dress code that players must wear "togs." The image of myself dressed in chartreuse pants is more than I can bear.

Confession time. I have been known to attire myself in Harley Davidson motorcycle riding togs prior to mounting my hog for a day of tooling down the highway.

You know, all black leather with chrome studs, buckles and fringe all around type togs – nothing pretentious and noticeable like those golfing slacks!

Okay – and here you may audibly sigh – one more thing I won't do in this life or any other. This has to do with a personal code of ethics.

I won't make canvas transfer prints of my paintings, hire a bunch of trained "highlighters," engage them to sit in my gallery putting little dots of paint on the prints, call them "personalized prints" and charge you 10 times what a dot-less one would cost.

Of course, without that pesky code of ethics thing, I could undoubtedly amass great wealth in the dots-of-paint business and hire people to defend me from people who laugh derisively at my Harley leather outfits or – not to discount any possibility, however remote – my chartreuse golfing slacks.

It's Bluebonnet Time in Texas

If you're any kind of artist, especially a painter, more especially a painter of traditional landscapes and you ply your craft anywhere within the proscribed borders of the Great State of Texas and you expect on random occasions to actually market your work, turn it into income for yourself and your family, well, then, you must paint bluebonnets!

Yes, you have to paint bluebonnets. There is actually no set number of the pretty little blue flowers that actually define a "Bluebonnet Painting," though it's been my experience that a mere one of the flowers seen anywhere in the scene makes it official.

I usually show more than just the requisite one in my spring landscapes – there are more than 5,000 different kinds of wildflowers which are native to our big state, but the ubiquitous bluebonnet is what we are famous for having.

Tourists all want to know if they are blooming and where they can be seen. These poor people sometimes travel all the way from Minnesota or Michigan or Iowa just to scope out our fields of bluebonnets.

I feel those folks, deprived as they are of naturally flowering landscapes, really do deserve to see and enjoy some of the wonderful spring scenes rampant in our Texas Hill country – rampant, that is, in a good year which this one is, thanks to well-timed rains last fall and just last week.

So, the flowers are out there, and I have been scoping them out. I have seen some really excellent patches of bluebonnets and primroses with nice accents of yellow Englemann daisies all along the Hill Country roadways, and I plan a trip to the Willow City Loop this week. I've gotten a report of a plethora of flowers in that area.

A good year in the Enchanted Rock-Llano-Fredericksburg country is a good year, indeed!

If one chooses one's flower tour day with care, one can avoid the big crowds of "sniffers" and can really soak up the beauty of the Texas spring landscape. I make the same statement about the Texas fall landscape, by the way.

Let me say to tourists and lucky Hill Country residents, in case you haven't been able to take a driving tour of our flower country this year, or you took a tour and missed the flowers, give my gallery a tour.

I have been painting furiously for the past month, creating what I think are accurate and atmospheric works on canvas and paper which celebrate our glorious Bluebonnet Time, fulfilling once again my honor-bound, moral and philosophical obligation as a resident Texas artist.

Some of the paintings do not actually contain a preponderance of Lupinus Texensis, but must still be referred to as "bluebonnet paintings."

It really doesn't matter what you call 'em, I suppose, as long as you can look and enjoy.

By the way, just for some of you Michiganders, I plan an upcoming work which will feature fields of white prickly poppies, growing so profusely as to resemble a snow-covered field you're more accustomed to – possibly at the same time in April. Snow up there, flowers down here.

Mother Teresa in a Cinnamon Roll!

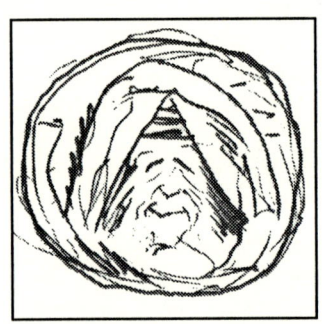

Mother Teresa in a cinnamon roll? Now that is truly a miracle!

How could you argue that it's not? Even if you are philosophically, politically or dietarily opposed to the cinnamon roll itself, and give them no credibility at all as medias of communication, the actual physical image of such a revered and renowned religious leader appearing on such a lowly and common food item must be taken as a miracle.

Though I myself was not an in-person witness to this phenomenon, I observed the image as did millions of other rapt watchers on television one night a few weeks back, and it was just as clear as could be. And we know TV doesn't lie, don't we?

Mother Teresa's aged, sublime countenance was there, peering from under her trademark head covering in such detail that we viewers could make out her wrinkled, beatific smile there in full display in the dough, the cinnamon and the frosting.

Well, I say, a miracle is where you find it, and is definitely in the eye of the beholder. As:

The Mother and Child, seen by thousands on the side of that 6 story glass building down there in Florida.

The Virgin Mary seen by I don't know how many in that tree stump somewhere in San Antonio.

A fuzzily realistic image of the face of Christ in a water stain on a wall in somebody's dining room. I can't recall where the house was, but I do recall, it was seen by several people.

Now at the risk of sounding facetious – I've run that risk before – I want to tell you about my own recent sighting.

This particular image may not, in some minds, qualify as a genuine miracle, possibly due to its subject, but in my eyes at least, it nonetheless should be listed as a Class II miracle – a minor one, a junior miracle, if you will.

Be that yardstick as it may, a miracle is still a miracle, is it not? And if you'll promise not to laugh or make fun, I'll share this marvel with you.

On the floor of my garage, directly under the place I park my Harley, I've discovered, in faintly smudged leaked engine oil, viewed from a certain direction and only in natural daylight from the opened door of the garage, there is, if one's mind is set to just the right wave length – that is, open to seeing miracles – a really good likeness of Elvis!

Yes. The sideburns, the smirk, the under-the-eyebrows smoldering look that sets females atwitter – all there. On the floor, it's the King himself!

I swear.

Are you laughing and making fun?

For shame, politicos

"Politics is the province of moral *invalids*" . . . who knows, but; ibid, op.cit, anyhow.

We in the corporate offices of Different Stuff, Inc. have begun to feel a little nervous of late. We are worried that we might actually hear a politician state his own goals if he is elected or even talk to us wary citizens about his own qualifications to hold such an elective office as governor of Texas or senator or representative from our state. That would indeed be something we would be unprepared to hear – a positive message from a candidate.

We don't know about you, but all we can pick up on our televisions and radios are ugly, mud-slinging, negative diatribes from each guy who wants the office. Witness the dirty, backstabbing tactics coming from both camps of the governor wanna-bes. Whoever we might have originally favored – the "sneaky" incumbent or the "sleazy" opposition – at this point in the campaign, we're hoping that neither wins.

It's a shame that these two supposedly mature adults seem completely unable to present themselves with the least bit of dignity. And we have to assign blame squarely on the shoulders of the candidates themselves. It would be far easier to fault their advisors and campaign managers. In the end, however, the man himself is responsible and sadly so.

We have always been disappointed in the way politics in Texas has been conducted, beginning way back in the days of early LBJ and continuing through Connally, Ms. Richards, that ole' boy from Uvalde, as well as the two oil guys from Midland. Can't we do better?

To answer our own question, apparently not.

This season's campaign – including speeches, photo ops and advertising – encompasses grappling – seemingly desperately – clutching, groveling in the dirt, wiggling down into the muck in a despairing, despicable search for some rumors of scandal to accuse the other guy of participating in or being responsible for.

We are not really surprised by any of this; we've seen it before though not to such a contemptible degree. This political season has established new, profound lows in the political process, prompting our acceptance of today's beginning quote. We are indeed more certain than ever of the veracity of that statement. A certain "moral invalidism" is being displayed by every candidate running for state or national office.

In every case, the opponents are being accused of everything but poisoning their own mothers. They are being vilified and being raked over the coals to an unprecedented degree in 2002.

What's the deal? Does anyone know?

Is being governor or senator worth making yourself look like such a low-class, common rumormonger as these two candidates for governor are doing?

Is spending millions of dollars slinging mud at another person – who is probably a well-meaning, decent fellow like yourself – just to obtain a short-term job which pays only a fraction of what you are dispersing from your campaign war chest to get worth it?

Anyway, we promise to vote for the first candidate who tells us in explicit language exactly what he stands for – and never mentions the other guy. He'll get our vote if he just stands up and explains why we should elect him instead of telling us why we should not elect that other bum – we already know that.

Gigs for Geezers

"Somebody asked me the other day, 'What do you do?' 'I amuse myself by growing old,' I replied, 'It's a full time job.'"
                                            Paul Leautaud, 1907

If, as the man says, you are in the process of "amusing yourself," then you will discover a raft of new activities you can participate in which will help entertain and beguile you as you begin your inevitable slide into antiquity.

These are things not recommended for young people at all. The capacity to enjoy such harmless pursuits is not within the province of youth. You gotta be well into geezerhood to really appreciate these things.

(We define geezerhood as that age when we first notice we cannot do ONCE what we used to be able to do all day long.)

But, there are many, many fun things we are still able to do in our advanced YEARS. Here are just a few, in no particular order of their enjoyment quotient, but rather in our usual haphazard fashion of listing stuff with those ubiquitous little black dots:

· We can have endless discussions with other, equally geezerly people about our management of various ailments and bodily functions. We have these things in common with many survivors of the state of youth and these discourses can be very educational as well as entertaining.

· That activity for geezers is usually followed by intensive debates over the merits, or lack thereof, of various supplemental health insurance policies available to us Medicare recipients. More fun!

· One of our favorite Old Person things to do is gather in a group of like-minded codgers and direct some moral tongue-clucking and finger-shaking at young people – all young people. Will they ever get anything right?
This same clucking and shaking is also great fun when directed at all current and prospective politicians, unless, of course, they happen to be fellow geezers.

· Reading obituaries. This, naturally enough, is a favorite pastime, a hobby, even, of ours as it gives us a certain gratifying assurance that, since we are reading the obits, we are not being read about. Imagine our distress should we discover our own name listed!

· For times when you are with a group of very close, intimate and perhaps even broadminded geezers, no activity affords more pure delight than liniment rubbing. "Right there!" we moan, "that's it!" we sigh.

· We recommend this one as a daily activity – porch sitting. We begin everyday with a coffee porch sitting session, preferably at sunrise. And it's a good day that ends with a wine or beer porch sitting at sunset. We find this daily routine, which youngsters don't have time for, can lead to a really satisfying time of doing another of our favorite gigs for geezers:

· Ruminating. This activity, in spite of the implication that it requires brain activity, actually doesn't, we find. To do some really good ruminating, in fact, one has but to let the mind drift (easy for geezers) and before we know it, our brain becomes occupied with relating, admonishing, justifying, reviewing, perhaps some regretting, even some solving, all of which come easily to the "high mileage" mind one acquires upon achieving geezerhood.

Stud Muffin Dove Foiled by Feeder

Return with us if you will to the days of yore – no, not "yore!" We don't have the vaguest notion what "yore" is or when it was, so forget that!

Let's just go back to last November when I described in a column the Stud Muffin Dove, a wily, overbearing bully of a white-wing dove I called "Arnold Schwarzendove" that drove all the little birds away from the plates of food we set out on the rock wall behind our house.

He was very territorial, was old Arnie, and remains so, though he is now suffering a major setback in his continuing efforts to rule the roost.

You see, we've devised a strategy, as all dedicated adversaries do, to gain the advantage over our opponent – in this case, the big, bully dove.

And we believe we've accomplished that purpose, in that Mr. Arnold Schwarzendove, aka Mr. Clint Eastdove, has been thwarted in his attempts to hog all the seeds for himself.

He is extremely frustrated. You can see it in his expression, his body language, his total agitation.

He flies in, he sees all the little wimpy birds happily feeding themselves, he tries to intimidate, he swaggers around on the wall, he huffs and puffs, he blows himself up to twice normal size by raising one wing side-ways to his tormentors, but to no avail.

They just go on stuffing themselves with the delicious sunflower seeds, ignoring the agitated antics of their aggressor.

All the oppressed group are there – the titmice, the chickadees, the finches, even the lowly sparrows – contentedly pecking away, leaving the feeder only when they have eaten enough, oblivious to the threats and bluffs of Schwarzendove/Eastdove.

What did we do? What strategy was finally successful in defeating the Hulk? We put up a feeder 10 feet away from the rock wall:

The Stud Muffin studies the situation for a while from his vantage point on the wall, swaggers back and forth while casting red-eyed glares at the feeder filled to overflowing with luscious seeds being devoured by puny little chickadees and sparrows.

He mutters to himself about the injustice of it all, puffs out his chest, flies over to the feeder and perches on its roof.

Mr. Big Shot then crooks his head sideways, sees all the feeding activity not six inches below his perch, but for the life of him, cannot figure out how to get down there to chase these little runts off and take the food for himself.

Study him for a moment. You'll be able to actually see that question mark appearing in the air over his head.

News From the Cloning Front or Back

Boy, science is fun! And the science of cloning is way out there "ahead of the curve," right there on the "cutting edge" in the continuous and convoluted search for eternal life – outside of religion as the answer, that is.

We humans need to have hope and some of the more pragmatic among us are counting on those pesky science folks to fix us up with a bunch of new body parts as our old ones wear out. They're working on it, we hear.

"Lab researchers make human kidney from cow's ear" is the most recent bit of news from the new Parts Department at the Human Repair Shop. (That's a brand-new franchise business being launched, we hear, by Howard Hughes Enterprises.)

Imagine it, if you can! A fully functional human kidney, manufactured from cells originally belonging in the ear of a cow, implanted, we suppose, into an actual human. Don't tell me science is not a creative art!

In our continuing efforts to help publicize and praise any advances in the various fields of scientific endeavor, we have, with some effort, awakened our Cousin (thrice-removed) Goober (we poked him with a stick) and inveigled him once again to compose a Lite Limerick on the subject of cloning. He acquiesced with this bit of doggerel:

"I wish I had some new knees
Rebuilt with some cells from mon-kees
Human kidneys were fused
From cow's ears that were used,
So why not new knees from mon-kees?"

Goober then collapsed from exhaustion, resuming his REM slumber.

We have given a great deal of random thought to this cloning business over the years – ever since Dolly the Sheep, in fact- and have reached several tentative conclusions, among which are:

If you can dream it up, some pesky scientist will try to do it.

We don't think absolutely all human beings should be cloned. We have an extensive list of persons who made the "verboten" honor roll.

Should a human be cloned successfully, this new person should combine as many good qualities as are available at the time. We also have compiled a list of what those particular qualities should be, along with the names of some people who have them.

Of course, this means that no one person has the complete course of good stuff, so we'll have to use cells from several different specimens in order to produce that Perfect Human Being.

What's that you say? That Perfect Person has already been produced? Some time back, you say?

Well, then, never mind.

The Different Stuff Driving Monitor

It's high time, people, high time – even maybe past time – to once again point out what bad drivers you are. All of you? Pert'n near all of you, as my grandpa used to say.

Good Driving Habits, or GDH, have all but disappeared, become obsolete, faded into history. The decline of courtesy behind the wheel began, we think, with the advent of the ubiquitously pervasive SUV, or Silly Useless Vehicle as they're known among the tiny, but thoughtful, segment of the population who don't actually enjoy aggressive driving or any other form of macho behavior and who, additionally, are still clinging to the old-fashioned ideas of fuel economy in their vehicles.

But, we digress. This column is directed to you people out there on the highways and byways who seem bent on having it your way at all costs – whatever vehicle you're driving. You know who you are.

You TAKE right-of-way, you do not YIELD right-of-way.

You do everything FAST.

You TAILGATE the car in front of you.

You make INCORRECT turns.

You don't ever COMPLETELY stop at stop signs. You do "country stops" even in town.

You CUT CORNERS when making a left onto the side street.

You pay MINIMUM attention to your driving – and these may be your worst habits, and they apparently are habits, as we see no improvement – you are still:

· Herding your vehicle with a cell phone stuck to the side of your head, thereby giving perhaps 35 percent of your already diminished capacity to paying attention to other drivers and the rules of the road and 65 percent of your attention to whatever incredibly important conversation you're having that couldn't wait 'til you could stop your car.

· Eating, drinking, shaving, putting on makeup, smoking, even reading while zooming along in traffic, oblivious to the fact you are inside a two or three ton armored, gasoline-filled projectile which could easily maim and kill your highway mates. (You would no doubt live through it, being oblivious and all.)

· Lastly, but not leastly, your attention deficit disorder is not assuaged or diminished at all because you are ANGRY. You are in a nearly constant state of upset because you are not able to always have it your way.

There seems to be somebody always in your way somehow – "What are those idiots doing on my highway, anyhow? Can't they see I'm in a hurry? Get outta my way! My 18 foot long, 8,000 pound, 40 gallon gas-tank-filled SUV with the Caddy Cruncher front bumper and monster tires is much bigger than that ordinary car they're driving. Move it! I gotta get to the gas station before I pick up the kids and go to the grocery store!

Boy, oh, boy, the nerve of some people who don't sit up nearly as high as I do."

Next week: Aggressive parking – five new ways to be in control even in a parking lot –

1. Taking two spaces with one vehicle.
2. Angle parking between straight lines.
3. Ignoring parking lot lines altogether.
4. Putting your 18-foot SUV in a 14-foot space.
5. How to avoid people whose car doors you've scratched.

Uncle Willie's Christmas Card

Dear Billy,

Well, son, it's been a while since I've writ to ya, but I want ya to know that all us geezers up here at the home think about ya now and agin and we 'preciate you visitin' us ever so often.

We all decided that we're not "Senior Citizens" at all. We're "Geezers or Duffers" or even "Old Fellers" and even once in a while "Old Poot" will do. See Billy, we ain't goin' along with all this "politically correct" foolishness – call a thing what it is, is our thinkin'.

Anyway, I woulda plumb forgot it was gonna be Christmas soon if I hadn't been reminded when I seen that there salad shooter ad on the TV the other day.

Thought about orderin' one of them things just fer the fun of it, but Nurse Kratchett reminded me we ain't allowed to have nothin that's got a sharp edge on it.

That woman's a real pain sometimes, but us old fellers agree she's kinda cute, in a macho kinda way.

I see the "White Light" salesman has done his Boerne sales run agin. They got them things strewed from one end of town to the other and they look real nice, too.

But maybe some wild-thinkin' person'll put up some colored lights this year – maybe some red or green ones, a blue one or two.

Talkin' about Boerne, I hear it's getting' to be a regular big town now days – got lots of stuff all the big towns have – traffic lights and jams, high prices, crime, a real police force to handle it all.

Lots of weekend tourists goin' up and down Main St. stirrin' up the dust mites that's on all that old stuff in all the stores. "Anteekin" they call it.

Well, Boerne is closer to San Antonio than Fredericksburg, I reckon, so them anteekers don't have to drive so far to get covered with dust mites.

And, ya say Boerne High School's got another good basketball team. Ya know ol' Stan'll git the best outta his boys, don't ya?

The kids'll play their hearts for him, just like always. And now, the school's lucky enough to have Rob Shivers a-coachin' the JV team – hear they doin' great, too.

Reckon ya musta been paintin' a lot lately, Billy, just like always only more so, huh? Got a surplus of them nice little pictures fer yer annual Christmas show.

How long you been a-doin' that, son? Ever since ya been in Boerne, I know, and some years before then, too.

Me and some of the other old timers here at the home are gonna make the trip down to yer place the 14th and see if we can drink up yer cheap wine. (If Kratchett'll look the other way for a minute or two!)

We would ask her to come with us, 'cept she does take up a lot of room.

Say, Billy, I sure do like the sketch you did of me the last time we visited. You know, the left profile where I'd combed my hair real nice?

Yer a good kid, Billy, even though ya ain't got a lotta sense.

Merry Christmas to you and yer far better half. I'll write again if I can remember.
Uncle Willie

Is Paradise Affordable?

Do you ever want just to up and run away from it all? Does your life seem pointless and drab? Do you wonder if there is some meaning and value to the sum of your efforts?

Is there even one answer you can count on to any of your questions? Hmmmmm?

Better yet, can you think of even one little question nobody's asked before? Betcha can't.

I suppose if you've never felt like running away from it all, you've had the perfect, Pollyanna existence, above and beyond any semblance of everyday reality. Hooray for you.

And, if that's the case, what I'd like you to do, you perfect Pollyanna person you, is to write down your secret and send it to Different Stuff. We'll market it and get rich. Then as rich people, we'll have some better options when we decide to run away from it all.

We can get on a cruise ship, for example, and run away from all by taking a five-star sail around the world or to Tahiti.

As rich people, our status assured by our possession of The Secret, we can buy our own spaceship and launch ourselves into the stratosphere and beyond so we can explore the outer reaches of the universe. Or something.

With the proper marketing techniques, and with me as CEO of our new outfit, our possibilities for getting away from it all are boundless, limitless and infinite.

Should we arrive at our particular pre-chosen paradise and find it somehow falling short of our expectations, why, we'll just move on to the Plan B Paradise.

All it takes is money, you know, not to give away any part of The Secret, but I probably just did.

We know that, speaking of money, there is only one thing it won't buy – poverty.

We also know that money can't buy happiness, but it can sure put in lay-away.

And even though money cannot supposedly buy happiness, it can sure make your misery more comfortable and bearable – maybe even enjoyable.

We at Different Stuff, however, experts that we are at nearly everything, can make no claim to knowing anything about money, other than our observation that if your life is pointless and drab, with money you can at least dress well and look good as you live your meaningless life. And if you feel like running away from it all, you can do it in style.

I've heard it said – by my ownself, matter of fact – that people are the same wherever you go. The only thing that changes is the scenery. Now, that is meaningful only if you don't mind knowing the same kind of people you've always known, but with different scenery around them.

So, we can unequivocally recommend having a few dollars in your pocket before you decide to up and run away from it all.

That said, after marketing The Secret and going public with our stock and our company goes belly-up and we're threatened with humiliating jail sentences, I will still be able to run away from it all because, you see, as CEO of the outfit, I'll receive a generous severance package which will help take the edge off any public embarrassment I may feel.

I say "may feel" because I'll be rich enough to hire people to feel embarrassed for me.

All the News That Is

It has been a week chock-full of cogent observations from the Different Stuff team of Crack Reporter – cogent and literate, too, those sometimes colorful utterances.

It seems that the reporting staff had been casually perusing the Big City newspaper on a recent Sunday. That's something the staff rarely does, apparently preferring ignorance to most of the information blatantly printed in the various sections of that big-time gazette. But interest was piqued by some published oddments, such as:

· The city manager of Hondo was arrested for possessing a marijuana plant in his home. Well! This poor, misguided soul was released on $1,000 bond and put on "administrative leave," whatever that is.

· A class of middle schoolers up in Missouri somewhere were advised by their English teacher to bombard a classmate with jelly – yes, jelly! – for refusing to take part in a reading exercise. They were subjected to disciplinary review by the school board. "It was peer discipline," said the teacher. Hmmmmm.

· This item strikes the staff as odd, too, if only for its headline. "SUV hits two Schertz officers." The staff wonders if the item would even have rated a headline – or a byline – if the two unfortunate officers had been struck by a mere car.

Perhaps, thinks the staff, their injuries might not have been so severe. Those crunchers everybody puts on the front of their SUVs would be most unforgiving in a confrontation with a human body.

Now, here are a couple of items written up in the same big city daily which cover a somewhat controversial subject: religion. But first, the reporter wishes to issue a disclaimer. We Different Stuffers continue to hold firmly to our lifelong, cemented position on any subject pertaining even remotely to religious acts and activities of total and complete fence-riding neutrality. We are maintaining NO position in our well-known efforts to raise NO hackles. We only report. We do not dissemble. Okay?

· Televangelist Benny Hinn is cruising right along, according to an article in the paper, flicking his wrist at believers, a movement which knocks them for a loop, but heals them of all sorts of dreadful ailments at the same time.

The silver-haired evangelist – aren't they all silver-haired? – recently moved his multi-million dollar operation to Dallas where he plans to build – what else? – a 50-acre, $30 million Theme Park, if donors can be inveigled to come up with that much scratch. Meanwhile, work is progressing nicely, reports Rev. Hinn, on his new $3 million house out in La-La Land.

· All the Baptists in the country – both the Southern category and the what? – the Regular segment – are in an uproar over some statements made by Southern Baptist Convention President Jerry Vines about the Jewish-Arab conflict, saying it is a war against the devil being waged by the Jews. He also called the prophet Mohammed a "demon-possessed pedophile."
Well, the Rev. Vines succeeded in offending absolutely everybody – Jews, Christians and Muslims.

We at Different Stuff will admit to a grudging, low-grade admiration for the oratorical skill it took for the reverend to, in one sentence, offend all the religions in the world as he declared his disrespect for other's beliefs, saying that those "other" religions are the cause of many of society's current problems.

The rabble is certainly roused now. We love a silver-tongued, and silver-haired, orator, though, don't you?

Advice From Aint Harriet

It's high time ya'll met my Aint Harriet – Great-Aint Harriet to be exact. She's Uncle Willie's sister and, as he is, from the ancient dinosaur generation which holds strong beliefs about life and how to live it.

Lord only knows how old the dear little lady is – she says she stopped counting her decades after her eighth one, saying, "A lady doesn't reveal her years after she's done 80 of 'em."

The old gal is pretty feisty and full of beans, as you'll be able to tell as I relate her latest bit of advice – verbatim wherever possible. Her language is, to the chagrin of the whole family, sometimes colorfully descriptive.

Aint Harriet writes in her flowery Victorian hand, "It's time the younger generation is made aware of the fine old art of snuff-dipping.

"I see these young folks cram a couple of fingersful of snuff haphazardly into their maws then spit on the ground, and it just distresses me mightily. Whatever happened to grace and elegance, I ask you? And discretion and refinement?

"Please let me acquaint all you snuff aficionados with, yes, the old fashioned but tasteful rules of dipping snuff.

"You'll need the following equipment:

"Either a one-pound coffee can or equivalently sized tin can. It is best, and very refined, to crochet a cozy for this can, since you'll be carrying it with you wherever you go.

"A lollipop stick, preferably wooden.

"A rounded ball of cotton, appropriately sized to fit inside your cheek without producing too large a bulge.

"A bottle of Garrett's Snuff. This high quality product is in powdered form perfect for genteel dipping, and we are only interested in gentility, after all.

"Now, for the proper snuff-dipping procedure. First, attach the ball of cotton to the end of the lollipop stick. Your own saliva will hold the stick and cotton together.

"Next, open the bottle of Garrett's, being careful not to inhale as you do so. The snuff is ground to a very fine dust ("corral dust" Willie calls it, but he has no class at'all!) and will certainly cause you to sneeze.

"Thirdly, wet the cotton ball in your mouth and dip it gently into the snuff bottle, twirling carefully until it is thoroughly covered with the brown powder.

"Remove it slowly from the bottle with one hand, and with the other, pull your cheek out to the side to accommodate the cotton ball.

"Ah, there, just perfect! The flap of your cheek presses the lovely ball of tobacco-soaked cotton firmly against your gums, and you are all set to enjoy.

"A word of caution for any novices out there. Do not swallow under any circumstances.

"If you should accidentally do so, immediately rinse and swallow with a moderate grade of bourbon whiskey.

"And don't forget to spit in your coffee can – as discreetly as you can, of course."

The old doll makes some good points, don't you think?

Yard Sculptures – A Critique

In this column, I will deliver a scathing commentary on sculpture for yards. I am qualified to do this because I own a beret. The criticism will not cover the following:

· Marble reproductions of Rodin's "Thinker" or the two-figured piece "The Kiss," two popular sculptures ordinarily placed in flower gardens.

· Cement birdbaths full of fluttering finches – common yard decorations.

· A Henry Moore abstract stone piece (with holes) mounted by the front entry.

· Semi-realistic concrete deer or ducks or rabbits or that slyly smiling pig people like to scatter in clusters around their yards.

· A life-sized pair of pink plastic flamingos posing gaily by the front sidewalk, even though this one is making a comeback as yard sculpture.

As I said, none of the foregoing will come under scrutiny this time, but your reviewer reserves the right to comment scathingly on them at a later time.

There is, difficult as it may be to believe, a modicum of taste, even class, in people placing a concrete deer in their front yard. Compared to today's objects of criticism, that is.

The same could be said about the plastic flamingos, I dare say, in that those particular articles are at least intended for yard decoration. The taste and class thing in the flamingo instance is, I guess, a stretch, however, and while we as neighbors may not be exactly enamored of them, we can be consoled by knowing of the intent.

But on to the object of disdain for this week. These so-called sculptures can be found in front yards all over Boerne, and the world, too I suppose – shamefully, unesthetically, blatantly, tactlessly to the extreme.

They are definitely not tasteful items of yard sculpture. No. These objects are:

A '93 Chevrolet Caprice or,

A '91 Honda Civic – red or

A '79 Ford half-ton pick-up. With rusted wheels.

Could even be, shockingly, a brand new $24,000 vehicle, sitting there on the front lawn.

Bad enough? Wait. It can get worse, and does:

All of the above yard sculptures clustered together in one grand heap in one front yard! Want to hear worse yet?
All that mess is on display for days at a time in a front yard very near you! Maybe even next door!

(Note to realtors and other sellers: the assessed value of the property with the sculptures, as well as those properties in the vicinity, is not, as you might suspect, increased by the addition of this "art-work." Contrarily, the properties all have lessened "street appeal," therefore, lessened value.)

"Don't get me wrong. I like my vehicles, too, and I've even loved a few, but for what they are – useful transportation. If I did own a $24,000 vehicle, and had a garage to keep it in, bet your life, that's where I'd keep it!

Call me crazy, but there's nothing in my garage that's worth $24,000. Not even my collection of half-full tin cans with dried paint them. Nor my swell assortment of cardboard boxes or my lawnmower or all those unidentified things there in the corner.

Well, "there oughta be a law" against such tacky and unsightly displays – there are still neighborhoods where the majority of residents take some pride in maintaining an attractive "street appeal" about their homes.

Of course, for all I know, these exhibits of metal, paint, rubber and glass may not be intended as "objects d'art." The owners may be in the used car business and are merely displaying their wares.

If so, I apologize for my criticism. I wouldn't want to be accused of being anti-entrepreneurial.

Stuff from the Round File

Just like the CIA or the FBI, I've been going through the garbage – the old "round file" as it's known in homes and offices throughout the country – and, as occasionally do our intrepid national law enforcement agencies, I've garnered some evidence of a possibly incriminating nature.

The round file (it actually is round) next to my desk more often than not contains notes I've made on random thoughts occurring at odd moments on widely diverse subjects, then discarded, for whatever reason.

A random sampling of my trash can exploration follows, after I issue a cautionary note to you readers that some of my discoveries were originally discarded because they were ideas "before their time." Others were the opposite – outdated.

But, we can rustle around in this effluvia and perhaps retrieve some items of topicality. And risking sounding like a troubadour of microscopic epiphany, I unwad the following scraps:

· The commonly used phrase, especially in these sensitive 90s, "live-in lover," engenders very little respect, does it, for either participant in the arrangement, man or woman.

· Society is paying a heavy price, it seems to me, for apparently having lowered expectation of our children. Many teenagers are in trouble because no one expected more of them.

· Why are people still smoking? (I ask perennially.)

· Same-sex marriages offer one sure-fire answer to over population.

· Cloning is another answer, it would appear, since no sex at all is required with this technique to make human beings. Even though new and different types of human beings would be a thing of the past – we'd have only repeats of the types we already have. Like them or not.

This cloning thing, though, begs lots of discussion and will get it in days to come no doubt.

It has another obvious advantage as is stated in this particular unwadded scrap of paper just retrieved from yonder file: it's a certain method for having "safe sex."

Far afield from the foregoing –(garbage is randomly recovered. I told you that.):

· Dignity is measured in "shreds." Guilt is "monumental." Peace is "lasting." Evidence is "overwhelming." Truth is "eternal." Joy is "boundless."

You can think of other units of measure, I'm sure. How high is up, for instance?

· Why are poets always placed in corners? You know – the Poetry Corner? Are we prejudiced?

Do we not really understand what they're saying? Are we embarrassed because we don't, and hope nobody will notice if the poets are in a corner?

Does anyone care what they're saying? If a bad or nonsensical poem is put to rock music, people somehow give it credence. And get rich on it, sadly.

Which reminds me of my cousin Goober the Poet. He's right over there in the corner and has penned this prime verse for us:

> *Pray, do recall whenever you are opining*
> *That every cloud must have a silver lining,*
> *It may be as easily avowed*
> *That every silver lining has a cloud.*

That's how sitting in a corner with cobwebs all over you affects your thinking.

The Altitude Theory

Our crack Different Stuff staff researcher has come up with an almost credible explanation for the voting machine fiasco in Florida. You've heard about it, haven't you? The repeat of the voting debacle of 2000? The same stuff is going on there now – déjà vu all over again.

The researcher presents a seemingly plausible explanation for the "lost votes" so common in Florida and other flat seacoast states as well. You have to think about this for a minute:

It's the AIR that close to the ocean. There's way too much oxygen for the human brain to assimilate efficiently, hindering really clear thinking.

As a result of this surfeit of oxygen, there is lots of sluggish thinking at election time, lots of memory loss. They forgot about the 2000 election already, those folks.

We like this theory and we can extrapolate that the coastal regions of the country do, indeed, seem to be run by what you could call the "fringe elements." Look at California, for example. Doesn't get much goofier than that.

An added factor, says our researcher, is that Florida hasn't got one mountain – not even a hill – where one could climb to the top and meditate to clear one's mental cobwebs, so to speak.

On the other hand, continuing to expand the theory about

oxygen, or lack of, look at a state such as Colorado. Lots of high altitude within its borders causing the opposite effect on brain cells. Oxygen-poor air, as has been medically proven by many other researchers, begets irrational, disjointed and even nonsensical thinking. So, we could assume that, according to the Altitude Theory, zero altitudes might be the root cause of typical conservative political policy which seems to emphasize wasting gigantic sums of taxpayer money on bloated, inefficient MILITARY programs while very high altitudes seem to give birth to your typical liberal political policy which seems to emphasize wasting gigantic sums of taxpayer money on bloated, inefficient SOCIAL programs.

Yes, there are exceptions. Oregon, for instance, is a regular bastion of liberalism (my word, those people up there are BIG on recycling!) And we must mention Idaho, which has a great many altitudinous areas, but has become a veritable stronghold of fundamentalist conservatives. (Too many potatoes, perhaps?)

Here's what our researcher (the crack one) has to say about Oregon and Idaho: while Oregon has a coastline, the state also has an abundance of high places, many of them directly at the coast, thereby creating an altitudinal IMBALANCE.

As for Idaho, abounding in altitude though it is, there are many valleys in the state where some coastal air has settled – it's right next to Oregon. Another imbalance.

Besides, there are abundant hiding places in both states and we can never know what sort of political theories are being developed by denizens therein.

A postscript to the Altitude Theory: we've noticed an inordinate number of moderates originate in the states across Middle America – moderate altitude, moderate political philosophies. No radicals either way in Kansas or Iowa – average altitude, not too low, not too high.

science & other stuff

Well, those pesky research scientists are at it again. Researching apparently 24-7 to come up with more stuff to put us all in a worry mode or, in the case we'll review today, a silly mode.

We'll do just a little worrying, too, of course. We'll be wondering who's paying the huge salaries commanded by these research scientists. Also, who is it that thinks up what to research? Listen to this latest, up-to-the-minute, real scientific discovery: caffeinated SOAP! You heard correctly – bars of BATH SOAP laced with caffeine! I can hear your first two questions. "What!" and "Why?"

Go back and re-read the first part of the last paragraph for your answer to "what" and hang with me a moment for the answer to "why."

You know how we're all in the time-consuming, if necessary, habit of getting out of bed in the morning and heading for the old coffeepot?

Then seeking out a chair on the deck or in the kitchen and to sit sipping the magic brew, anticipating the moment the caffeine kicks in and you can begin to function mentally and physically in an almost normal way? You need that caffeine, don't you? Your daily existence is dependent on that critical first cup.

Those pesky researchers, banging their heads on their Bunsen burners in their continuous search for new, time-saving devices and products, can now save you from all that precious time spent lollygagging over those morning cups of coffee.

Get your hit of caffeine right there in the morning shower. No more need to waste time in a muddle waiting for the stuff to travel from the stomach back to the brain. Just wash your head with a bar of caffeine. (We'll discuss what to do with your saved time in a future column.)

Now for some non-science. This next is by way of congratulations to Elena Tucker who writes "Off the Main" – you know, right there across the page in our very own Hill Country Recorder.

She wrote an excellent piece a couple of weeks ago (Sept. 18, I believe) titled "A World Away." I want to thank her for it. I really couldn't have said it better.

Longtime readers of "Different Stuff" can tell you that cell phone users have, from the beginning, been one of my pet peeves – nay, more than a peeve – people who live their pitiful lives with that electronic appendage attached to their heads. They are at best inconsiderate of the rest of the world and at worst a menace to public safety.

You said it best, Elena. It's so sad to realize that we have only the "here and now" and cannot truly be "in the moment" when we are constantly "being in touch" electronically.

My own existence is devoted to enjoying the physical world around us and celebrating it in the best way I know how – in paint. I regret all those moments of distraction that happen.

We'll just have to keep on sidestepping, dancing out of their way. We can't stop it – even little kids have the addiction to punching numbers on little machines.

Imagine the size of human thumbs in future generations! And the diminution of human brain cells!

You Knew it was Bound to Happen

The following columnar commentary has absolutely no factual foundation at all, and has not been researched by any crack staff of research personnel, either.

It's just another crack-pot notion that occurred to me one day as I was mushing some oil colors together, preparing to apply them to a totally blank, but apparently receptive canvas challenging me from my old easel.

The notion: Is it possible to replace me with some kind of machine? Could a computerized mechanism of some sort do what I do? Will I become obsolete as a singularly unique human being?

Be honest. It's occurred to you, too, hasn't it? Your job can be done by some mechanical monster, some technological device which is much cheaper to keep than you are, and not nearly so apt to break down.

At this very moment, as we are surmising, pondering this possibility, there is some nerdy little guy in some obscure little cubby hole designing and constructing a high tech apparatus which will replace you or me, lock, stock and barrel.

We will then be obsolete. Who needs us, anyway? You and I are mere humans, subject to every conceivable form of frailty which can cause work stoppage.

We are way too expensive to maintain, and we soon wear out,

anyway.

The nerdy little guy in his obscure cubbyhole knows this, so he is busy at his task of fabricating an appliance which feasibly will replace you and me.

A really good case in point: The Big Blue defeated world chess champion Gary Kasparov last week in a highly publicized match which had all of humankind trembling in fear.

The Big Blue is, of course, a computer – a super computer, if you will – capable of literally overpowering the brain of a brilliant human being who had never lost a chess match before.

That really hurts, doesn't it? A superior human mind literally overwhelmed by a collection of wires and bits of plastic! It's depressing, I tell you!

The little nerdy guy is patting himself on the back over there in his little cubbyhole, muttering to himself. "Hah! Now, for that smart alecky old artist out there in Boerne, Texas.

"How hard can it be to paint an oak tree and a field of bluebonnets? I'll soon have a machine that will paint the perfect oak tree and field of bluebonnets. Then we won't have to put up with that curmudgeon and his so-called eccentricities. We'll have perfect paintings and no problems of upkeep."

So, people, it would have been better if I'd kept this particular notion to myself, right?

Uncle Willie Rides Agin

Dear Billy,

I ain't talked to ya in a long time, young fella. How ya been keepin'? I been a-crippin' along purty good myself, I reckon, considerin' my age and bad habits! Ha ha!

Them bad habits surely hurt ya, Billy – like our grampa usta say, "if I'da knowed how bad off I'd end up, I'da took better care a myself!"

I'm also findin' out somethin' else the old bugger said ain't exactly true, though – "you kin do what you've always did, long as you keep doin' it!"

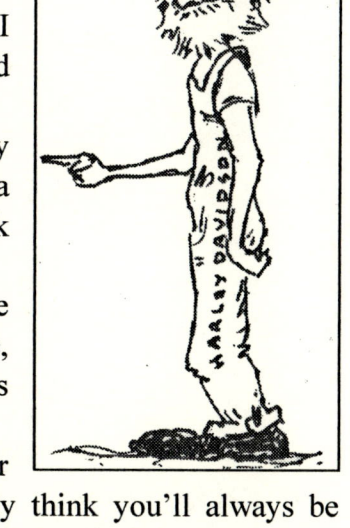

Not always, I'm discoverin'. For instance, take yer Harley. You probably think you'll always be able to kick it over and scoot on down the road on it. Maybe you can, thanks to electric starters! As another of them old sayin's goes, "May you have the ability to take yer virility into yer senility!"

Speakin' about Harleys and scootin' down the road, you may not know that I myself climbed aboard my own motorcycle and headed up a gang of riders back on the first of November. We done a five-day ride out to Big Bend and there abouts. They was nine of us to start, includin' one young sprout name of Blinky. He was a ridin' on one of them BMWs or "Big Machine fer Whimps." All the real cowboys was a-ridin' Hawgs, although some a these new models is too purty to call "Hawgs."

They was the original Los Amigos, Less One. Ol' Zorro was missin' but Teddy Bear and Zep was there to keep up the decibel level. And Ol' Snake, he come along so's we'd remember just why we do these rides – oglin' the ladies, dancin' at ever opportunity, ridin' fast to get there sooner to commence the evenin's drinkin' and oglin'.

And Ol' Uncle Willie, of course, along to try and keep up a semblance of sanity and organization, though them things ain't yet ever happened.

I'm about to swear off ridin' in front, though. Them fellers do a heap of complainin', but I ain't heard no offers to take over ridin' point.

We did have a rousin' good time, though, in spite of the gripin'. All the boys – Flaco 'n' Cruncher 'n' Hooter 'n' two raw recruits, Phil and Paul – claimed, as did us veterans, it was a bang-up time.

We stayed at some fine and fancy hotels, including the Gage in Marathon where I personally got no sleep at all 'cause of the railroad tracks a-runnin' smack through the middle of my room. Then there was the Chisos Mountains Lodge – real purty – the Antelope Lodge in Alpine – so-so – and the Limpia Hotel in Fort Davis – real nice.

We ate regular and good and had some good ridin' in between, with no bike problems – purty good fer there bein' 10 bikes.

The evenin' bull sessions are always a lotta fun, all that joshin' around, 'specially since they was a couple of "virgins" along – two fellers who'd never been exposed to all the infernal nonsense as goes on on the Los Amigos bike rides. The two a them – Phil and Paul – are purty well broke in now. We're workin' on handles fer 'em right now.

Oh, yea, Billy. Yer old Unc Willie did try to raise up the cultural level of this Harley Posse by pointin' out some a the places in Big Ben where you've did paintings. Tried to point out the artistic aspects of the great big country.

We also had a brush with some real art education from Phil, the sculptor, over in Marfa where some New York artists have nearly took over the town, like some space aliens. Ya done good, Iron Man.

After a 450-mile, butt-achin' ride back home, all the fellers'll be tellin's some more lies about the ride. You don't have to hardly beg 'em a-tall either. This here's a pitcher from the trip, Billy.

Vroom, vroom.
Uncle Willie

The Day the Earth Moved

On Oct.12, 1999, the number of human beings crowded together on our poor overburdened earth home reached the astronomical number of 6 billion souls!

That's the very day the earth moved, tilted, shifted on its axis. The weight of 6 billion people has finally caused the planet to spin in a wobbly fashion.

Six Billion! Nine Zeros! That's double the population since the 1960s. Imagine that. According to those pesky (and extremely busy) number-crunching demographers who keep track of this kind of stuff, it took the first couple of million years of human existence to reach 3 billion bodies, then only 34 years to double that. Incredible.

The imbalance of weight which is causing the axis to wobble is due to the enormous birthrate in China and India, both on the other side of the earth – though it's also getting a little crowded right here in downtown Boerne, too.

Old Mother Earth is groaning and creaking under all this added weight – earthquakes cracking the surface, volcanoes erupting from the added pressure, El Nino, droughts and floods – all indications our overweight little planet is tilting a little bit off its accustomed orbital habit.

We first really noticed it on Oct. 12 – though we were waiting for it to happen – when the very delicate imbalance occurred, it's believed, over in Southern Europe: a bouncing, earth-tilting baby boy, eight pounds something was born. Just enough weight to start things wobbling.

As I write this stuff, my crack staff of researcher is on assignment pestering the scientific community to come up with a better theory than the one I've been espousing to explain more scientifically the above-mentioned disasters.

They are also looking for explanations for the world-wide rise in mean temperatures which apparently has caused a gigantic chunk of ice to break off the Antarctic shelf now floating north where, if that baby melts, we're liable to be living on the beach without having to move from Boerne.

How about that? We could be beach front property owners and not have to move.

And all because nobody's told all those people who are having babies one after another exactly what causes them.

Oh, there are some who know what causes babies, and lots of them are – insanely enough – taking fertility drugs.

Well, the added weight on the already-hefty Mother Earth certainly will only add to the wobble problem. And I've not even touched on the other obvious problems caused by overpopulation – pollution, starvation and way too much traffic on Main Street.

But listen, it gets worse.

Those same number-crunching demographers have predicted that the population of our world home will double again by the year 2030. We ain't ready for that, no way.

I have a stock tip for you though. Buy any company that makes deodorant.

Senility – A Near Miss?

The rule seems to be: forget half your stuff on the trip To, then forget half of what you remembered to take with you on the trip To on the trip From so that when you get home, you find your stuff pile is down to one half what you had before the trip To and after the trip From, one-fourth of what you had at the beginning.

Huh?

Okay, let me try to simplify it. If you take very many trips To and From, you'll eventually end up with a finite pile of stuff that is not nearly as much stuff as you used to have.

That wouldn't be a bad thing, would it? Don't you have way too much Stuff? Lord knows, I do – most of it formerly very valuable Stuff I thought I couldn't possibly do without.

Worse even than holding on to all that stuff is thinking you have to carry a lot of it around with you on your trips To and From. Which brings us back to where started – forgetting stuff.

Some of you dear readers may be familiar with my semi-thought-through theory that, as we age, we do not lose our memories. We merely attain Total Brain Saturation or TBS. That's a condition of antique brains mostly, though young brains, too, are occasionally affected, wherein we have no more space in our cranial cavities for even one additional bit of information, fact, list, duty, obligation, appointment, name, face, location, number, address or what have you.

The storeroom is full. There is no vacancy.

If any new info does manage to penetrate, an equal amount will have to be ejected – which makes it fairly difficult to lose an old geezer. Like a trail of breadcrumbs, just follow the discarded brain memory cells and they'll lead you right to him.

All of this is not news, of course, to us geezers and geezer watchers. With a modicum of adjusted thinking, we all can learn not to merely cope with the situation, but to actually enjoy it.

We don't have to remember stuff because (1) nobody expects us to and (2) we'll continue to perpetuate the "memory loss" myth.

It's a much more stress-free life when you forget your stuff. It was way too hard trying to keep track of it anyway.

And now, with less stuff to remember, we can go on about the business of having a good time doing stuff which occurs to us at the moment – like little kids.

We can enjoy our "moments" a lot more now. Like a goose, we can awake every day to a brand new world free of stuff we thought we wanted to remember from the day before.

We forgot yesterday. You know, all those bits of stuff we had stored up are now like motes of dust, settled on the earth. Dust to dust?

So there you have it. A light dissertation on the foibles of so-called memory loss, which, as we at Different Stuff have observed previously, doesn't happen only to the old guys. There are lots of young people who have contracted "pre-senile dementia."

These folks also go around forgetting half of the stuff they wanted to take on the trip To and then forgetting half of the stuff they did remember on the trip From so that they, too, end up with a finite pile of stuff.

Here's the difference between them and us, though. They'll replace their forgotten stuff. We won't. We can't remember what it was!

Ready for Winter?

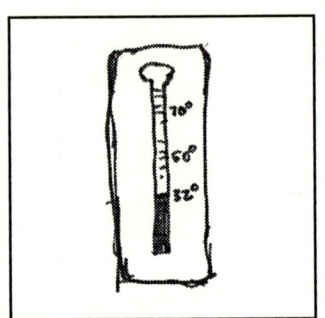

We're never ready for Old Man Winter, are we? And answer me this – why is winter called Old Man Winter? Why not Old Lady Winter? Or Middle Age Guy Winter? Old people do not enjoy winter, do they? Boy, I don't.

I put in my time in Cold Country as a young man and I can tell you I've had all I want of snow and ice and long, dreary days trying to keep warm.

Down here in South Texas, we are never quite prepared for that Arctic air nonsense that gets blown our way nearly every year about this time.

We just naturally become complacent as we enjoy our T-shirt Novembers. These extremely rude invasions of cold from northern Canada are hardly welcome.

It always happens so suddenly. Last week's episode was typical. Monday we had coffee on the deck in the morning in pajamas and light robe. Another libation in the evening on the same deck, wearing T-shirts and swatting mosquitoes.

Then came Tuesday. I hate it when the morning temperature will be the high for the day – 55 degrees in this case. With the temperature steadily dropping as the day goes on, the bones are thoroughly chilled by Tuesday evening.

We denizens of South Texas make no preparations for this event, even though we know it's coming – inexorably. The first of the annual, infamous Blue Northers will bear down on us sometime, we think, but not soon, right? Maybe next week. Or next month wouldn't be so bad. Just not tomorrow.

That's how our thinking goes year after year and it's why we're never ready. So we have to hustle around in the cold, putting our plants on the porch and constructing a temporary – we hope – greenhouse to keep them from death by freezing.

We have to make sure our furnaces and stoves are in good working order. Why didn't we do that stuff when it was warmer?

Our vehicles need to be winterized, of course, but I'm not as worried about winterizing my stuff – plants and stoves and cars – nearly as much as I'm worried about winterizing myself.

That gets to be more of a problem every year. Every Blue Norther that blows in makes me more and more certain that the majority of us human beings are just not suited to withstand any temperature below 72 degrees Fahrenheit.

Occasionally, you'll hear somebody say, "Oh, I'm glad it's cooling off. I like cold weather." Hummm.

Let me say this: those folks who purport to enjoy cold weather fall into one or more of the following categories:

· They own long underwear and insulated gloves and, perhaps, a fur coat.

· They own a ski lodge in Colorado.

· They are very young and have never had to shovel sidewalks and driveways or walk three miles to school on top of a frozen crust of snow three feet deep, then back home slogging through a couple feet of semi-frozen slush. Uphill both ways, at that.

· They have broken, non-functioning personal body thermostats which give their brains false temperature readings.

I say these people should live in Minnesota and we could watch them on TV shoveling the snow off their buried Hondas.

That's my kind of winter-blizzard-watching—on TV in my T-shirt.

some questions we'd like answered

*"Knowledge is proud that he has learned so much;
Wisdom is humble that he does not know more."*
William Cowper, 1785

Isn't life funny? - to get right into the questions.

We were thinking that as we wend our way along the torturous trail of life, being fairly attentive and alert to our surroundings, that some actual answers would occur to us. We age, if we're lucky, and we gain experience as we survive each day and, supposedly, our wisdom grows proportionately.

It's been said – no doubt by people who are in the business of saying wise things – that the wise man knows how much he doesn't know.

Boy! Are we Different Stuffers wise! For instance, we don't know, don't have the beginning clue to answer this one:

· According to all available evidence, Adam and Eve were perfect human beings, made in God's image and all . . .so where'd all the ugly people come from?

No answer is forthcoming there, so we'll ask another.

· Is a mechanical dog as fulfilling to the soul of an old person as a real one? Some say yes – except for batteries, they're pretty low maintenance and they're guaranteed flea-proof.

Okay, that's sort of an answer, but we're not entirely satisfied with it.

Let's move along in our search for answers to others of life's persistent questions:

· Why is it you never hear a person jabbering on a cell phone say, "I love you?"

· If a man is alone in the woods and does anything at all, is he still wrong? (Of course he is, is the answer!)

Another question that persists:

· Why do all the crazy, goofy, nutsy, gun-totin', government-hating fundamentalists want to live in Idaho? Same reason they seem to cluster in Montana?

· Why doesn't John McEnroe just do the decent thing and disappear? Who ever gave him that television job should disappear with him.

Here's a couple of bothersome questions we've had on our minds for quite a while on subjects automotive:

· If the car makers can give you a $6,000 rebate on a vehicle, what does that say about the margin of profit they maintain?

· What's the thinking behind the Cadillac PICKUP?

There are also a multitude of perennial boy-girl questions which actually came up in our early adolescence, but are continuing to this day and seem no nearer to being answered than ever.

· Do women actually think it's attractive or cute for men to wear earrings? We stupid guys must believe they do because, I guarantee it, we do not wear 'em for each other.

· Why is it that women's sense of humor is so different from men's? We try our best, as do most men, to appear amusing to women, but with only moderate success. Is that because much of guy humor is based on bodily functions?

We have but one more question pertaining to the male-female situation, followed by a typical guy follow-up statement:

· Why is it a scientific fact that women have better verbal skills than men? By way of answering that, we say, "Duh!"

Rampant Crazy Stuff

"Truth is more of a stranger than fiction."*

Yes, you human race, you. You're at it again. You have such imaginations. You are so inventive.

If it can be thought of, you can and will do it, no matter how goofy it seems or how senseless or dangerous or destructive. There are things, no doubt, that even you haven't thought of yet that will soon be added to your repertoire.

We will be watching, appreciating and reporting such as:

· One of our perennial favorite things you crazy nuts have been doing for we don't know how many years is the annual and sometimes deadly Running of the Bulls in Pamplona, Spain. This activity rates near the top of the scale of crazy things to do and you are surely familiar with it.

Spain, as you know, is the original land of spicy food, hot Flamenco guitar music and romantic, bloody wars and equally bloody bullfights. On the first day of the national sport – sport? – of bullfighting, the day's herd of bull steaks are let loose in the narrow, winding streets of the ancient city of Pamplona and are herded toward the venerable bullring at a dead run.

A crazed, probably drunk, group of young men – and an occasional, equally crazed or drunk young woman, if you can believe it – runs along the streets directly in front, not in back, of the maddened, thousand-pound, sharp-horned bovines for I don't know how many blocks. Many of them end up gored, bruised and busted up for their efforts.

The television camera people have a ball, the injured or killed runners achieved their 15 seconds of fame and the bulls are all killed slowly in the ring by guys with sharp sticks. Sound like fun?

Ready to take his place on our all-time Goofy Stuff List is our latest hero-cum-nutwad, the Wimbledon Streaker.

This is our kinda guy. Just when you thought the art of streaking was becoming passe, viola!, the man of the hour, literally, in our minds at least, saved Wimbledon from one of its most unsatisfactory finishes ever. Really. Are we a little bored with watching those sisters taking turns trouncing each other?

So the Wimbledon Streaker has our vote for membership in the Goofy Stuff Hall of Fame. He's a sure-fire winner.

I have been remiss in not apologizing for the Different Stuff Rain Dancers. In their eagerness to alleviate our drought, the dancers overdid it again, causing the recent deluge.

I told 'em to slow down, go easy, but there's no stopping the dancers once they get into it.

Remember the '98 flood? That's right. They gave it too much that time, too.

On the subject of floods, this last downpour revealed, right here on television, another of our candidates for Dummy of the Month. This was the guy – ashamedly we must acknowledge the preponderance of Goofy, Silly and Crazy Stuff is committed by GUYS – who went merrily across enormously flooded and choked with debris Canyon Lake at the height of things astride his jet ski.

We got to witness this Stupid Thing as did the governor of Texas from a bird's eye seat in the helicopter carrying the Gov across the flood area.

This guy gets the coveted Stupid Prize awarded periodically to that fringe member of the human race who performs the most imaginatively dumb thing we can imagine.

We seek self-explanatory, if obscure, quotations.

Pardon Me While I Harken

Once in a while, it's fun to employ an archaic word or expression in one's speech, if for no other reason than to record reactions from one's audience. Bafflement, bemusement and befuddlement are common responses, along with an attitude of chagrin or pique.

"You smart aleck," they'll say, "I bet you don't know what that means, either!"

Well, don't get mad at me. I'm a geezer, remember, and I was raised in an era that taught respect for our own language and reverence for those who learned it well.

My mother, as I may have mentioned before, was indeed a stickler for the proper usage of English. If a word wasn't spelled correctly, pronounced correctly or used correctly in a sentence, then it simply was wrong. We did not use contractions or otherwise butchered words such as "rite," "lite" or even "thanks" for "thank you."

I must say that one does become lazy about one's speech, though. We take shortcuts, I think, because no one thinks they have time to listen. We have become a nation of people with what I'll call "Attention Span Deficit Disorder," or ASDD (I do love acronyms.)

So, I believe people are missing one of our most pleasurable activities when they go around grunting at each other, not making eye contact, ignoring the conversational possibilities between live human beings in favor of one kind of electronic communication or another.

Readers are familiar with my views on the cell phone culture. But that's another column.

The initial impetus of all this harkening was the realization that I have never had any sort of "crisis counseling." I had never heard of such until just the last few years and it got me wondering how in the world I and my contemporaries ever made it through all the various crises of our youth without it.

Perhaps we did talk things over with a family member or a friend – I think that's what we did because we did know how, after all, to talk. We were able to express in concise, accurate verbiage how we felt. And further, we were gifted listeners because these were skills we learned from our mentors.

My harkening back made me nostalgic for some of the good old days – not all, but some. Those revered, hazily remembered "good old days" were, of course, not always good.

But, as to language skills, yes, the old days were good. I will confess, however, that I never achieved much expertise in the pastime of "chatting." Idle chit-chat. Talking to hear yourself talk. Passing the time of day, so to speak.

I'm afraid that TV ad about beer which has all these guys in a bar asking each other, "Howyadoin?" and answering each other the same way – "Howyadoin?" will become a way of chatting – total non-communication, no exchange of ideas or thoughts at all.

Look out, folks. It is said that we will lose it if we do not use it. Talkin' 'bout our brains here, dude, like, you know . . howyadoin'?

The Sad State of the Arts

Let me explain about the print over there to the left. So far, it has cost you only the price of the newspaper to look at it, but if you'd like to bring it to my event, I or my highly trained, certified Highlighter Person will scatter several dots of actual paint at crucial places on your print – even as you gasp in awe – then, we will charge you, with a nice smile on our face, something like $479.68, plus tax, for your now personally highlit print. When it's dry, you'll be able to feel actual paint dots, just like you would on a real painting! Exciting, huh?

Warning: there will be, of course, 286,411 other paint-dotted prints just like yours, though not all of the owners got to witness, personally, the actual highlighting with paint dots, so you're ahead there.

Note: the fantastic scene described above – it ain't gonna happen, folks, sorry. But, unfortunately it IS happening in the world of art more often than is comfortable for those few purists of us left. We who do and purvey original works of art are entirely dismayed by the dotted-print flood. There's a veritable avalanche of highlights out there.

And there seems to be no stopping it. More painters all the time are getting on the paint-dot bandwagon. Copycat events are mushrooming.

One cannot help but admire the hugely successful commercial aspect of the phenomenon. There are some really big-time PR people doing some really big-time PR, that's for sure. And some highlighters are getting big-time rich.

Okay, so be it. I, as one of those almost obsolete dinosaurs who persist in the art game, will no doubt continue in my pokey, old-fashioned way to produce, one at a time, the very best possible original paintings, pushing myself to the best of my abilities, the top limits of whatever skill and imagination I can muster. You can be sure I will remain true to my lifelong belief that art appreciators, buyers and collectors deserve only my best and ORIGINAL efforts.

There! You can take the preceding paragraph as the closest thing to a guarantee I can give you.

Art reflects life, they say, and it becomes increasingly difficult for this old Geezer of Art to accept how easily people in art – buyers and sellers alike – have been able, even willing, to lower their standards about defining art, then rationalize to justify that new definition, "it's what people want." they'll say.

"First, I'll make some money, then I'll produce the art I want," is another excuse which holds no water in my mind. I assume that these folks are all sleeping well at night, too, especially after making that large deposit at the bank.

So, perhaps, art does reflect life, after all. At least life as we know it – we do accept less than the best, don't we, and call our lives "good."

Over the past few years, I've noticed I don't have any "young" students. Young people, say, kids under 50 – and the students I do have will bear me out on this – don't seem to care to learn the traditional art of easel painting like's been done since Rembrandt. Set a canvas on an easel and, after many hours of sketching, researching and composing, make a painting, usually with smelly old oil paint.

Attrition will have its way as it always does. (Sigh.) My kind of art will sadly pass into oblivion, along with the natural subjects I like to paint. But the high-lighters will persist so long as they don't run out of prints to dot.

Meanwhile, though, I do sleep pretty well at night, even though I made no large bank deposit.

Aint Harriet on Manners

Bill Zaner's Aint Harriet is the guest columnist for the week, commenting on social mores in her inimitable style.

Billy, I enjoyed a fluttering palpitation of the heart one day last week as I was dining in a restaurant of some local renown. And I say "enjoyed," my nephew, pointedly. Indeed, at my age, any variation at all in the area of emotional activity would be a moment to relish.

The reason for the palpitation, and let me emphasize that it was a pleasurable one, was that, as a family-mother, three children of varying ages, an older lady of the grandmother category and the father – was seated at a nearby table, it was to my everlasting stupefaction to observe the man actually remove his hat – a cowboy one, at that – and set it on an empty chair. This man remained hatless for the entire meal!

To further enhance my rapidly increasing pulse rate, the man, the totally hatless one, helped his wife and his mother be seated by pulling out each chair, then scooting them into position at the table and asking each lady in turn if the position was satisfactory.

My joyful amazement while observing this unusual spectacle of polite, old-fashioned courtesy nearly brought on an episode of the vapors!

It had been many, many years since I had seen a display of manners that we used to label as "ordinary" or "commonplace," especially by a relatively young person, male or female.

I really do miss what we used to call "common courtesy." Such was taught as a matter of course in every home by both mother and father. A child was drilled daily in what was called "proper" behavior and was expected to employ his manners in all his social situations.

Note: It must be said at this point that my use of the pronoun "his" is used in the old-fashion "neutral gender" sense, applying to both boys and girls. Remember, Billy? Before political correctness?

Unfortunately for your old Ainty Harriet, the instance of good manners I witnessed in the restaurant apparently was an aberration.

There were several other men in the place with their gimme caps and cowboy hats firmly situated atop their heads and I saw no other act of chair-holding displayed.

It served to bring me back to the awful reality that nice manners are seemingly on the wane.

It's sad, isn't it, nephew, that one sees more and more scenes, in the media as well as in real life, of totally rude and disrespectful behavior between people.

Speaking of the media, does it not cause you to wonder once again whether art imitates life or vice versa? But to be practical, what does it matter – the result is the same.

One's sensibilities are battered by the rampant crudeness depicted on television and in the motion pictures – a reflection, you can be certain, of real life.

And in return, the evidence points to a reverse effect as well –

real life is a reflection of celluloid role models.

A satisfactory solution, I believe, can only be achieved if each of us would adopt once again the biblical axiom, "Do unto others as you would have them do unto you." No one can possibly enjoy being treated with unfeeling casualness, can they, Billy?

This old lady for one will continue a lifetime of giving respect and demanding it in return.

By the way, my boy, thank you for walking clear around your pickup to assist me with the door and making sure I was properly ensconced therein.

Yours is a remote opener too, isn't it? You don't have to make the trip around to the passenger side, but you do out of courtesy and respect

Thank you for remembering your childhood training.

Love, Aint Harriet

Questions & (?) Answers

It's time once again for Mr. Answer Guy to clear up a few obscure, but pressing questions that hardly anybody ever thinks about asking. Perhaps more of us will begin asking some of the tough questions after Mr. Answer Guy lets us know what they are.

Question: Why aren't all the candidates for major political offices this year being arrested and put in jail if they've done all those dreadful things they are being accused of doing?

Answer: It's a lot easier for opponents to sling mud than it is to catch it.

Question: Would you yourself camp out overnight on a sidewalk so you could get yourself a donut?

Answer: No.

Question: How about a ticket to a rock and roll concert?

Answer: Are you nuts?

Question: Why do the words "flammable" and "inflammable" mean the same thing?

Answer: Next question, please.

Question: How many banks does one little town need?

Answer: At least six.

(Note: Mr. Answer Guy has never claimed publicly that he was any kind of financial guru, although he did let it slip that he'd advise investing in so-called "hard goods" such as nice, big oil paintings.)

On to the next question, a two-parter: What, exactly, is a "compliance inspector" and why does he drive a Range Rover with "compliance inspector" painted on the doors?

Answer, sort of: Let me first define "compliance," directly from Mr. Webster, the first Answer Guy: "giving in to a request or wish; a tendency to give in to others." Okay, so if you don't comply, you get a mad inspector on your case.

(Note II: We asked the AG if that was the best he could come up with. His answer: yes.)

Question: What about the Range Rover part?

Answer: Beats having to drive an '87 Yugo.

Question: What motivates television producers to make stupid sitcoms such as nearly all the new shows this fall?

Answer: There is a serious shortage of actual working brain cells in that business.

Question: What's the thinking behind the new Hummer SUV?

Answer: See previous answer.

(Note III: Mr. Answer Guy thinks the car makers should employ him to name the new, bigger monster vehicles. He would stay up nights, he says, to do the job and his nicknames would be much more descriptive – the Hummer Pulverizer. Now that's catchy! Or, to call a spade a spade, the Chevrolet Crusher. Avalanche doesn't sound threatening enough, says he. Another: the Cadillac Blaster. Much more befitting to a Caddy, he thinks.)

Last question for this session of informative Q's and A's: Have you thought about how all those thousands of "downsized" SBC employees must feel about that zillion-dollar basketball gym?

Answer: Yes, I have.

Question: Well?

Answer: Let me answer your question with a question. Have you ever been polled? Are your answers being used to count percentage of approval, for example? Were you asked what you personally thought about dropping bombs all over the world? Hmm?

A from Q: No, I wasn't.

Q from A: Neither was I.

Times are Tough (But Not All Over)

Times are not so tough, relatively speaking. Take, for instance, the following examples:

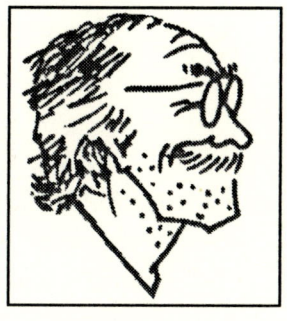

· The beauteous and irrepressible Liz Taylor spends a million dollars on a party at Disneyland to celebrate her first wedding anniversary with her child-groom. (She probably thought it was worth it – after all, a whole year!) The groom, in fact, when asked to comment on the big party, replied, "duh, right!" That was the same comment he'd made, reporters noted, when he was asked what it was like being married to a woman 25 years older than he.

· Could you struggle by on $390,000 a year? Plus perks and the best health insurance? Turns out that's the annual salary of the big boss of the United Fund. But, that's not all – he has condos in all the best places where the jet-setters go, and has been doing some heavy duty investing in profit-making ventures, and not for the profit of the Fund. Hmmm. Make you feel a warm glow about donating? Especially if you work for a company who puts pressure on you to make regular donations.

The straw-breaker, though, was when the local UF chief paid officer, (who gets only a pitiful $140,000 per), in a radio interview, claimed he didn't know how much the New York guy made, but that he was probably worth it, because he was such a good fund raiser, I guess!

· It's easy to see where our parents went wrong. They told us: "Go out there and get that education, boy, they can't take that away from you!"

What they should have told us was: "Go out there and practice throwing that baseball, and catching it, and hitting it with your bat! You could get paid $43,000 every time you play a game, boy, or, to put it in annual terms, you could get seven million big ones a year! And, the year's only seven or eight months long! You could retire to Hawaii by the time you're 28, boy! Think about it! Even if they do take that away from you, boy, you can go on strike until the fans get restless, and then get more!

An appropriate limerick from Cousin Goober:

There's an overgrown boy, don't remember his name
Whose job's playing baseball, 43 grand a game.
See, baseball's no quirk
For avoiding hard work,
He spits and he scratches for fame.

Note: The number TWO player, in a television interview seen by this reporter, was whining pitifully about how he thought he is worth more, really, than his bare subsistence salary of only $4.8 million a year. (Sob!)

Had I been the interviewer I would have shown a little more sympathy for him than his questioner did. After all, everybody knows that times are tough!

Out There on the Acoustical Edge

Does it seem to you more mature citizens of old planet earth that some of the edges have been moved? Extended? Pushed further out when you weren't looking? Or, in some instances, brought closer?

When you are pushed to the edge does it look like that line where your patience or endurance runs out is in a different place than you thought? Maybe it takes more to aggravate you these days – or maybe less.

Take noise not of one's own making, just for example. I'm thinking about how noisy the world is because of where I've been and also because I'm CURSED with almost perfect hearing.

Now, I am pushed to my personal line of endurance somewhat sooner than I used to be – it takes only a note or two from a passing boom box to press my trigger.

That stuff is awful, intrusive and obnoxious. And inappropriate out here in ordinary society. One can only be grateful that one is not trapped inside the car with it. Can you imagine?

The perpetrators of that racket will tell you when you complain, "if it's too loud, you're too old!" Boy, have they got that right!

I've just returned from a 2-week sojourn to Big Bend. Not the Big Bend of the Iowa tourists, the camp grounds packed with silver-sided vehicles jammed so close together everybody's aware of each other's bad breath and sleeping noises, but the Big Bend of the little-traveled dirt tracks, the back side, the quiet places. In a previous column I wrote how while I was there the Hale-Bopp comet's tail looked like it was 18 inches long, opposed to the maybe three inches it appears to be here.

Now, I can further report that the comet makes no noise as it zooms across the night sky. If it did, you could have heard it from some of the quiet, quiet places I stayed in the Bend.

I count myself extremely fortunate that I have experienced, many times in my life, such perfect silence. The places left on this earth where one can do so are, sadly, becoming much too rare. So are the people who care about such things. Rare.

So, the downside of experiencing such quietude is, of course, coming back to this edge of the acoustical world. It seems even noisier than before. And, after being infused with all that lovely silence, it takes some time to readjust to the cacophony of modern life.

Today is a sweet, quiet day, though, a Tuesday in spring in our nice little town. Quiet, that is, unless it's compared with that one primitive back country campsite in the far northeast corner of Big Bend National Park I inhabited a while ago – the one called Bone Spring Draw – where there was nothing between my watercolor palette and distant Nine-Point Mesa but clear, silent air.

I'm now listening to cars, airplanes, lawnmowers, barking dogs – typical, ever-present, perhaps even comforting to some – here in our nice little town.

Makes me wish even more for two things: personal space control buttons on boom boxes and a National Day of Silence.

Every week.

The Doctor Is In

"Y'all orter live yer life like they ain't no tomorra!"
Aint Harriet

Bless her crotchety old heart, Aint Harriet had all the answers. "You cain't go fer wrong," she'd say, "long as you foller my advice!"

Let this be fair warning, intrepid readers. We, ourselves, will soon open up our new practice in the wide open field of pop psychology. Indeed, just as soon as our diploma-by-mail arrives, we'll get it tastefully framed and mounted on our wall, put on a nice suit and commence our life-affirming, $100 an hour, formula-laden, softly delivered advice on how you people should find out who you are so you can live a better life.

We will adopt a catchy nickname, easy to say and remember, like, say Dr. Phil or Dr. Pill, or Lord help us, Dr. Bill. If we can somehow work it out, we'll get us a TV show where we can dispense platitudes and cliches on camera and look good doing it. (We'll need a large crew of top-flight makeup artists for that.)

Of utmost importance, and to give ourselves credibility with the gullible – and we expect only the gullible as patients – we will work out some sort of plausible-sounding formula with numbers, such as 10 life-changing events which have happened, seven ways to cope with those 10 life-changing events – we'll owe you three –

five important people with maybe 12 unimportant ones we will call Bozos.

We'll also attach a bunch of important sounding initials to the end of our name – always a crowd-pleaser. Let's see . .. .we could call ourselves, pardon the immodesty, Dr. Bill, DA, PDD, DGC, PDQ. You gotta admit, that's impressive – and worth at least $100 per hour, especially if we get to be on television for our very own 15 Minutes of Fame.

We've noticed – and that's our job as a journalist, to "notice" stuff – there is no dearth of so-called pop psychology around these days. Almost every one of today's crop of television talk shows has a more or less regularly participating counselor of the psychological type appearing at intervals on the program.

To a man, or woman, they have just worlds of good advice for all the viewers on exactly how we could straighten ourselves out and quit being such quivering blobs of stressed-out sad excuses for human beings – if we would just listen to their sound, book-learned advice.

Like all practitioners of the medical arts, however, we pop psychologists cannot give out any guarantees that our well-meant instructions for fixing up your miserable lives will actually work – unlike the man who sells you a washing machine, which, matter of fact, actually does make your miserable, dirty life a great deal better.

We will plunge ahead, though, and offer up a truckload of exhortations on improving yourself, including, without charge this first time, the fine advice offered to us some years back by our very own Uncle Willie, that wretched old soul, who rasped, "Keep doin' what yer doin' and you'll keep gittin' what yer gittin'!"

However, when you visit our fine, new pop-psych office with our brand new diploma nicely framed on the wall and we are wearing our nice suit, we will ask you to pay for service at the time it is rendered for you have no credit with us.

Jobs – the Good, the Bad, the Ugly

At the outset today, a clarification is called for: I personally have no practical working knowledge of jobs, only what I hear and observe.

This small treatise, then, will be based on fantasy alone since your intrepid Different Stuff author has never had an actual job, but, rather, has somehow managed to avoid anything resembling gainful employment for, lo, these many, many decades, no small accomplishment.

A small qualification might be in order, however, because being in the Army came close to having a real job, so much so I remained in the employ of my Uncle Sam for no longer than the absolute minimum enlistment, de-enlisting myself at the very earliest opportunity.

So what follows is a short list of jobs I don't want and jobs I wouldn't mind having, should this fantasy achieve fruition. All in no particular order of preference.

In my cowardly heart, not many occupations have such a high fear factor as high-rise window washer. We've seen the videos and photographs of these terrified guys clinging to the side of a skyscraper, dangling by a flimsy rope. Rock climbers? They're asking for it.

If this list were more of a stupid job list, near the top would be the occupation of bull rider. These individuals, having had all their brain cells rattled, shaken and stomped from their heads, have proven one thing for sure – there is no limit to human stupidity.

Probably the toughest, and maybe the most boring, of all jobs I don't want is plumber. Ever look at the hands of a long-time plumber? They show it all, don't they? Dirty, strenuous work, and I thank God for them.

Right up there with high-rise window washers would be arborists – you know, tree-trimmers. I watched some of these intrepid gentlemen scramble up and down and all over a big oak in my backyard cleaning out the ball moss and it was scary. A guy clings precariously to a two-inch limb 40 feet off the ground with a chain saw dangling from his belt, nipping bits of the ubiquitous moss with his two handed clippers. My breath caught in my throat. No thanks!

But the absolutely least desirable job I can think of, and one of the most dangerous, is driving a school bus full of middle school kids. 'Nuff said. On the other hand, here're a few pretty good jobs.

Pro golfer – and you all know my views on that silly pastime. But how else can you make that kind of money with so little time and effort.

This one has its hazards, but what kicks! Stunt pilot.

I really believe I would have made a good general of the army. Just think how much intimidation power you'd have – make lots of people jump. On the same line as general, only with much better pay, would be CEO of Enron. What a really good job.

One of the best jobs, however, which can result in a lifetime of accomplishment and satisfaction, if not great financial rewards, is the occupation of artist. Wait! That IS my job!

No, not job actually – more like hobby which appears to resemble a job, but which everybody knows has no actual work involved in it.

Ah, well. It's tough, but somebody has to do it.

The Suggestion Box

In our persevering, continuing, not to mention ongoing efforts to be of some service to the public in general and our intrepid readers in particular, we Different Stuffers maintain what we laughingly call the SUGGESTION BOX.

The contrivance is, of course open to any and all written recommendations by any and all people who follow the procedure set down by the DS Rules committee:

· All tips must be typed, double-spaced, in triplicate.

· All suggestions must be accompanied, in a sealed envelope, by a $20 bill.

· Strict hours for access to the suggestion box must be observed – between 2:35 and 2:40 am on even-numbered Mondays.

· Combination for the padlock is not available.

But, in spite of the stringent conditions, some proffered proposals for improving the condition of the world have managed to land on our desk here at the Different Stuff World Corporate Headquarters in downtown Boerne, Texas.

We, along with our crack staff of screeners, have sifted the lot, rejected the bulk of them, but are nevertheless left with a handful of what seem to us to be worthy ideas which could indeed help solve some of our society's most pressing concerns of the day.

We present the following ideas, with total neutrality on our part, for our readers' consideration only:

· This one is like closing the barn door after the horse got out, but, we sometimes can only learn the hard way. The idea here is to put rock bands' budgets to better use than pyrotechnics at their concerts – use the money instead for singing lessons.

· The next two suggestions – credible ones we think – have to do with better use of America's shrinking open spaces. The first advises us to develop the entire state of Nevada into one giant golf course, thereby relieving the rest of the states of their obligations to take up precious land with greens and fairways and clubhouses. We do believe, however that the clubhouses could stay.

· We like this proposal a lot. In another, remote and little-used state – North Dakota comes to mind – collect all the funds used for such purposes in the United States and build a billion-acre dirt bike track, again relieving all the other states from having to destroy perfectly good land for such a dubious purpose. Think of all the "passive recreating" that could be enjoyed by us tree-huggers!

· We like some of the suggestions that slipped through concerning "Reality" TV shows. Some shows should be produced that depict Real Reality – stuff people really do such as:

– International Shopping Competition.
– Fashion Model Ogling for the guys.
– Bachelorette Reject Assessment for the gals.
– Bad Driver Contest
– Multi-gender Nose-picking.

· Lastly, certainly not leastly, we have an idea which is overdue in our estimation and we present it with some trepidation.

Let America employ its own weapons of mass destruction wherever we deem it necessary. Present as gifts to whomever we're trying to destroy, a full-sized, monster SUV – the H2 Hummer jumps to mind – chockful of cartons of unfiltered Camel cigarettes. This would take a little more time, we know, but it would be just as fatal – one way or the other.

Stuff I Like to Think About

There are many things I don't like to think about – death, taxes, pollution, overpopulation, crime, disease, and traffic on Main Street. The list of stuff I don't like to think about is as long as your arm – as they say, a mind-boggling amount of unthinkable things.

The solution: a counter-list of pleasant and wondrous stuff to occupy the old brain cells, if just for a time.

Here's something: those pesky explorers of the unknown cosmos, astronomers, while scanning the infinite darkness one day, found a new, nearly parallel solar system. It's kinda like our own little sun and circling planets, they tell us, with a couple of notable exceptions. This new sun is huge, as are the three accompanying planets.

The one which corresponds to our earth – the "third rock," – is three times the size of our own rock.

This astronomical stuff is fascinating to think about. When one lets one's imagination loose on the subject, it becomes more and more engrossing.

Imagine, if you will, that all things on this new world are also three times as large. If there is a gravity pull of triple, then the human-like inhabitants of that planet would have to be 18 feet tall and weigh 600 pounds. Can you fathom, for example, dealing with a 500-pound, 16-foot tall mother-in-law?

Heck, Jesse Ventura himself would be probably 20 feet tall and weigh 800 pounds.

What an impressive sight – the shaved head itself would be the size of a truck tire. The glow from all that freshly-shaven cranium would require sunglasses to look upon.

Talking about truck tires, on new Planet X, the tires on your four-wheeler would have to as big and wide as your Buick. Imagine the beer cans rattling around in the bed of your giant truck. Two cans would fill up your recycling bin.

But big tires would be very useful in case a nine-inch cockroach started across the road.

Here's another neat thing to think about. Looking way into the past 360 million years ago with those pesky paleontologists, whales looked like hoofed coyotes, they say.

Yes! Paleontological (note the last seven letters in that word) evidence says that those creatures fed by the water's edge, gradually running out of water-edge-stuff to eat, so after a few missed meals, they wandered into the water – no doubt donning their scuba outfits first – to find food.

They soon found out they didn't need hooves in the water, so they realized the flippers in their scuba outfits were just the thing. Pretty soon, the flippers wore out, and they got together and decided they'd just evolve flippers right on the ends of their legs. Save time not having to put them on every time they wanted to go some place.

Obviously, we humans aren't as whales – we can't hold our breath for half-an-hour. And we still have to put on flippers if we want to use them to swim and dive.

But, conversely, whales don't have fat-tired, four-wheel-drive pickup trucks.

The Beach Connection

All us human beings feel a kind of genetic attachment to the ocean, I think, and most of us look forward to an occasional visit to the beach.

We can stand at the edge of the sea and feel the magnetism  of our roots. (Well, you see, some of those pesky scientists hold that our species first crawled onto the shore billions of years ago in the hopes of growing legs where we'd had fins. Those primitive creatures might have reassessed the situation, however, had they known how some of our legs would look!)

In any case, the appeal the sea has for us is undeniable, whether it's on board a ship far out from land or staring hypnotically at it from the shore. I've always said about the coast that "it's a nice place to visit, but I wouldn't want to live there." My limit of time for beach visits is three days – four is too long and two leaves me feeling slightly unfulfilled.

So a three-day visit to the coast serves me well enough to renew the ancient relationship, if there be such.

There remain a few rare places along the Texas coast where one can be alone with the sea, surf and sand, but even those are disappearing and that's so sad.

There was an aerial photograph in the San Antonio paper last Sunday showing the development that's taken place over the last decade or so on that narrow spit of land we know as South Padre Island.

Literally miles and miles of high-rise condos and hotels are built cheek by jowl, as close to the surf as they could get them, leaving no room for dunes to form a barrier.

How much time before the waves wash away the very foundations of those buildings and they crumble into the surf?

In February, we had occasion to view from the air the results of many more decades of development which has obliterated any sign of a natural seashore.

Florida's east coast looks solid with buildings for its entire length, again built as close to the incoming Atlantic waves as possible, assuring there is no natural shoreline at all.

There is some hope, however, for small bits of ocean shore to remain under developed, a few places where it's extremely difficult to erect a condo, although, we can be sure some developer is seriously looking into the problem.

I'm thinking of a half dozen places along the Oregon coast as well as the coasts of Washington and Northern California.

There are insurmountable cliffs in those places, hundreds of feet high, plunging directly into the ocean, leaving no room in many cases for a beach at all, and certainly no adequate building site. Then, too, some of that shore is included in the National Park system.

Which brings me home to Texas where, thankfully, a large section of Padre Island is protected from those ubiquitous developers by being included in the Padre Island National Seashore.

Most of this 70 or 80 miles of open beach can be traversed by car on most days and four-wheel-drive vehicles on "soft sand" days, not that you'd want to do that. It's really kind of boring – seen one sand dune, seen 'em all. But, one is able to achieve total solitude on that strip of beach – any time but Spring Break, of course, when a lot of the sand is covered with drunken teenagers.

There is, on a good day at the beach, for the sensitive soul who is looking for that hereditary connection with the origin of his soul, the possibility of realizing such an affiliation with the universal self.

It's worth a try, I think.

A Hero Passes

It's hard to believe he has died. The man was a genuine, real-life hero to me for as long as I can remember.

But he is not dead and gone. He was an artist and he produced his own monuments with paint on paper and canvas.

He has ceased to exist on the physical plane, but he remains so much alive in his work.

Some of that artwork hangs on the walls of my home and studio and has been there since the 1950s. I study the man's brush strokes and glorious combinations of color and never cease to marvel. The artist composed visual symphonies of lines and color. Wonderful and fulfilling they are – food for the soul.

He painted in what's known as the "traditional" style. That is, the objects depicted in his works are recognizable for what they are – trees look like trees, horses look like horses, rocks look like rocks.

But there is much to realize under the surfaces of his paintings – something profound and beautiful, something ethereal and poetic beneath the layers of paint. Soul. A piercing perception of the inner substance of all things natural.

There is an underlying statement being made about the condition of man and his world, things understood by the sensitive viewer.

One of the outstanding characteristics of this hero, maintained and practiced for his nine decades, was his full-to-the-brim sense of humor and his powerful sense of the ironic.

"We ain't gonna get out alive," he'd say, "so get that frown off your face!"

He possessed a great sympathy for all people and showed kindness for the lowly as well as the high-born. His human-ness and that ever-present and merry twinkle in his eye is what I miss already- there's not enough of that around, for sure.

I thank the powers that be that I got to see him just a couple of months back.

"Haven't seen you in so long I plumb forgot ya!" he regaled me. Then told me a joke, twinkling in the eye as he did. Sharp of mind and tongue.

He looked out the side of his macular degenerated eyes at one of my drawings I'd brought along – still looking for the master's approval – and told me it was "pretty durn good."

He asked me to read him a piece I had written and he chuckled over it.

He told me that he had to paint. You see, it's like having a disease you can't cure, an itch you can't scratch, and he still managed to "ruin about a painting a week."

Then he put both his hands on mine and said he was real glad to see me and it looked like I was doing just fine.

I don't know how many of us get to interact like that with our heroes. I don't know if young people even have heroes. Or if they are worthy heroes.

If heroes are people we want to emulate, be like, then I'd wish everybody could have my experience.

I'll never forget what he said to me on the phone back in December when I told him I was planning to drive out to Arizona to see him. He said, "Better hurry up, Bill, I am 93 years old, you know!"

I really miss you, Hal Empie.

April 10, 2002

Intellectually stimulating stuff

"Intellectually stimulating" is just a matter of personal judgment, isn't it?

The stuff I'm hereby presenting as such will probably not stir the brain cells of a bona fide egghead, although the possibility is that the thinkers of profundities just might be able to find a modicum of inspiration in even the homeliest of clichéd wisdom.

Emanating from that lump of bone atop my neck, these random thoughts – some read, some made up, some borrowed, some actually swiped – pop into mind at odd moments. Sometimes they leave an impression, sometimes not, nevertheless mulled and mentioned – "woolied" as my mother used to say.

Like: while it is apparently a statistical fact that male workers draw larger salaries than female workers overall, it is also apparently true that the fair sex has a larger percentage of the finances which move the country along.

The gals are therefore able and willing to tell us guys exactly how we should spend our bigger paychecks, so things, again, get evened out.

This situation, then, apparently creates a paradox, right?

And: (I stole this one) for relieving one's guilt about wasting food, the good old refrigerator does a good job, and you probably never thought about it before as a psychological appliance, did you?

Here's what happens – you ate a wonderful, delicious dinner, and boy, there's some left. So you put the leftover stuff in a container and put it in the refrigerator thinking, "That'll make a nice lunch sometime soon."

Time goes by and you forget about the stuff until one day you discover it's still in there, only now it has this fuzzy green growth on it.

Does that cause you more than a moment's consternation? No. You tried to save it. You could just hear your mother's accusing voice saying, "clean you plate, remember all those starving children in China (or some place.)"

Your effort was genuine. The refrigerator will take care of it. It won't be wasted, you thought.

But now you can pitch the fuzzy, greenish-coated stuff without guilt. See?

Also – can you really call it a vacation if you brought along your cell phone and your pager, fax machine, laptop?

And if you feel you have to check your e-mail every day or listen to the radio or television news casts, are you really having a vacation or just working in a different place?

As a person afflicted with good hearing, it's always been a concern of mine. Quiet places are more and more difficult to find. If you are so fortunate as to find some solitude, why would you bring your pager?

One more, from Mr. Buddha.

"If you understand, things are just as they are. If you don't understand, things are just as they are."

Oh well. These and other eternal questions and verisimilitudes keep coming up as I slide into terminal geezerhood. I do actually have a whole set of pretty good answers. It's just that they don't exactly match up with the questions. Speaking of questions –

This is probably one which has no answer, but I need to ask it, anyway.

"Mom, what do all those starving children in China (or someplace) have to do with whether or not I clean my plate?

How to be a Good Offensive Driver

Here are the basic physical items you'll need to refine the art of offensive driving:

A vehicle. Preferred machine is an SUV or "Stupid, Useless Vehicle."

This is the car of choice for most offensive drivers and is especially effective when equipped with huge, knobby tires which put you even higher and therefore superior to most other drivers – a definite edge.

Besides, an SUV equipped with 4-wheel drive and fat tires could come in very handy on your way home from the post office or school if you decide to do a little "off-roading."

Just leave the pavement and take off across yards and lots and knock down some bushes and flowers and small trees. It's even better if there's some mud.

Some essential inside-the-vehicle equipment would include: Makeup for you gals and an electric razor for you guys. It's important for good offensive drivers to carry along with them in their cars plenty of things to keep them occupied while bombing down the freeway – things to take their minds off the actual driving of the vehicle.

Applying makeup – eyebrows, lipstick, etc. – at 80 mph is a highly desirable skill, as is shaving.

Something to eat. Hot coffee (not too hot, of course, unless you retain a sharp lawyer), breakfast items such as donuts, cokes and burritos, all go down well at freeway speeds and are excellent distractions from the dull mechanics of steering and braking.

Smoking items. There's absolutely no reason not to smoke in the car. The mental distraction afforded by fooling with cigarettes while maneuvering through 5 pm traffic cannot be underestimated If you're a pipe smoker, so much the better.

Oh, yes, be sure to flip your butt out the window – the still-lit cig can provide a chuckle for you as it bounces off the windshield of the guy behind you.

Perhaps most of all, the car phone can be a truly wonderful tool for the offensive driver to provide long minutes of diversion from the mundanities of safe, defensive driving.

It is crushingly boring for the aggressive driver to practice those ordinary, supposedly good driving habits.

Now, really. Why should anybody actually yield a right-of-way? Take – no – DEMAND the right-of-way, people! And, for God's sake, do not ever, ever let another vehicle get in front of you.

No! Climb up his back bumper if he doesn't get out of your way – you are, after all, taller than he is, and your tires are way fatter.

In addition, you are on much more important business than he is, and those two minutes you'll save by being the aggressive, offensive driver you've always wanted to be can be put to good use when you arrive at work.

You can use that time productively to refill your coffee cup and have another smoke.

So gentlepersons, start your engines (and don't forget your eyelashes, your shaving cream, your munchies, your smokes and your phone) and have a good, aggravatingly offensive day – and be sure to flip 'em off when they drive the actual speed limit or less.

Take your Vitamin L

I'm still looking for that really special someone. That profoundly sensitive, intelligent and insightful person. That perceptive, understanding and hugely caring human being, a "soul mate," if you will. Who will above all things, laugh WITH me instead of AT me.

Most people have the skewed perception that I am an "object" of humor rather than a "purveyor" of it. If this situation arouses in any of you gentle readers even a note of sympathy, hey, you could be the ONE!

Never golf with an Almighty.

Are we all in this pickle? Do we all lack whatever self-esteem it takes to just shrug off ridicule of our personal personage? Do we all hope for someone to understand us enough to see through our absurd presentations and perceive the true and righteous and genuine humor underlying the facade?

Who cares?

The whole problem, like so many of our other problems, perceived mostly when we are young twerps, can be overcome by just outliving everyone who failed to get our jokes. Yes, that'll learn 'em, by golly! It is another benefit of seniorhood. There are few enough, I'll testify. But we'll take 'em as they come, like your basic 10 percent discount.

They say humor, a sense of it and the use of it throughout your life will and does prolong the process. Boy, am I hoping that's true! It is easier to make some people laugh than it is others, we know. Look at the people in the professional comedy business. They themselves admit they make the best audiences. Sort of like people who have tried to paint pictures are better at appreciating paintings.

Of course, ya'll know I'm kidding, don't you – about that soul-mate thing? I don't really care whether you laugh WITH me or AT me. Just laugh, okay? And laugh hard and long. Lord knows that there is plenty to laugh at out there in that silly world.

Here is something. Golf, a really hilarious activity, in fact, played by notably humorless people, makes the game itself pretty funny. Golf is the only sport God is known to play. A joke: He and St. Peter are out on a Sunday morning. On the first hole, God drives the ball into a water hazard. The waters part and God chips onto the green.

On the second hole, God takes a tremendous whack and the ball lands 10 feet from the pin. There is an earthquake, one side of the green rises up and the ball rolls into the cup.

On the third hole, God lands in a sand trap. He creates life. Single-cell organisms develop into fish and then amphibians. The amphibians crawl out of the ocean and evolve into reptiles, birds and furry little mammals. One of these furry little mammals runs into the sand trap, grabs God's ball in it mouth, scurries over and drops it into the hole.

Finally, St. Peter looks at God and says, "You wanna play golf or you just wanna mess around?"

And there you have it; your average daily requirement of essential vitamin L (for laugh), also known as your moment of silliness. C'mon, it can't hurt!

Different Stuff brought to you today by Bulb Nose Productions, 123 Laffaminit Lane, Chuckleville MO 123456.

Patriotism Reborn

Day Five. A lot of us were stunned into an unbelieving silence by what happened that horrible dark day of Sept. 11. We could not find adequate words to describe our feelings.

We stared uncomprehendingly at our televisions or listened with incredulous ears to our radios. We seemed to be doing our daily chores, going through the motions, trance-like, numb, moving about in robotic fashion.

Only now, five days later, am I finding some ability to speak. Of all the quantities of words I've flung into the surrounding atmosphere for all these long decades, I find no wise ones to put into my little weekly column in my hometown newspaper. There are no "silly moments" this week. I cannot produce levity and won't try.

I am a lucky man. We are lucky people. We are citizens of the United States of America. If you are not, you are probably striving to be and we will welcome you as an equal – you will be our countryman and we will stand beside you and help you. Nowhere else in the world will you be made as welcome as you will be here.

Most of us came from somewhere else. Originally, anyway. We're all mixed up, a lot of us, in our ancestry. There are more and more of our citizens, though, who are of one race only and lots of them are in the process of trying to gain citizenship. We will let them and welcome them.

We Americans have made and will continue to make some very big mistakes. It's part of our history as a nation. We've mistreated many people, we've been prejudiced, narrow-minded, even cruel to some of our own citizens, such as the harsh way we treated our Japanese citizens during World War II. We put them in prison camps just because they looked like our enemies.

Aren't we supposed to learn from history? Isn't that why we study it so we won't make the same mistakes? Are we about to make some of the same mistakes again?

I hope not.

But, we are angry, and we're ready to rip something apart. Revenge is what we want. We want to get hold of some perpetrators and tear them limb from limb. We are empowering our president and all elected officials to do just that.

Oh, yes. We're mad all right, furiously, blindingly so.

We can be hurt. We can be gotten to. Terrorism is not an abstract concept. It's not something we know about only by audio-visual communication. It's not a sound bite on the evening news. Not anymore.

So. We are Americans. We are rich and we are spoiled. We live very well, the majority of us, in our wonderful, open society. We are free. And I hope that we will always be free and open. Yes, rich and spoiled, too.

I am confident though that we will continue to keep our doors open to the rest of the world and that we will welcome one and all to our precious country, no matter who you are or where you come from. Unless you come here, take advantage of our good hearts and plan to hurt us.

Then we will tear you limb from limb.

September 19, 2001

Assorted Stuff, part 27

Politics:
I would have made a good politician and I'm about to tell you why; because I know how to take credit and receive accolades and pats on the back for things I actually had nothing to do with.

This skill is a good one for a politico to have. It allows you to step forward for congratulations whenever something good has happened on your watch, whether or not you had anything to do with it happening.

Take the economy, for instance. If things are going well for business – lots of Gross National Product, low interest and inflation and most of the common citizens (who's that?) are doing okay, e.g. not starving – then you, as a politico can step up, chest out, toothy grin and take credit for the good times.

You have to know when to lay low, too, though, as in when things aren't so good. Then you lay the blame on your esteemed predecessor. You may remember him – he was the swell-chested, toothy-grinned guy who was there during the last economic upswing. Remember?

Further Politics:
I was extremely disappointed about the vice-presidential debates not coming off the other night. I was looking forward to "My little brother can whip your little brother" fracas.

Social Stuff:
Watch out, all you cowboys. The Courtesy Police are

patrolling all the restaurants in the area, giving out citations to all you boys who don't remove your head coverings inside the house.
Weird Word of the Week
"Oenophile"
Meteorological Stuff
I love autumn. The weather. The colors. The nice feelings one has just being alive, especially we South Texans who've survived another hot summer waiting for autumn. We made it.
Jokada Week
There was this famous movie star in town making appearances to the delight of one and all. One of his stops was at a local nursing home.

The man and his entourage made their way down a hallway to the main sitting room where he stopped to talk to a little old lady sitting in her wheel chair, dozing a little, taking in the sun.

Mr. Big asked the old lady, "Do you know who I am?"

She gazed at him rheumily for a beat or two and replied, "No, I don't, but if you'd go to the desk over there, I'm sure they could tell you." (Credit Frankie Davis Glenn, all-around interesting lady.)
Jokada Week II
Speaking of nursing homes – the old man was to have his 90th birthday and a group of his relatives got together and hired a lady of the night to entertain him in his room.

The old guy was greeted by a young woman, who said, in her sexy, breathy voice, "Hello, Old guy, I'm here to offer you some supersex."

The Old Guy thought for a minute and replied, "I think I'll have the soup." (Credit Mary Alice Yelverton, another nice lady.)

If you have any jokes for me, write them on a $20 bill and send them to: ME.

Ye Shall Know Them by Their Bumper Stickers

Stickers on bumpers let the world know a lot about you. Besides, they are a source of amusement and information – usually useless information, but amusing.

Since we are duty-bound to fill in the gaps in the public's cultural awareness, we will offer some examples of this particular source of communication.

Politics are a favorite topic covering car bumpers. So is philosophy. Causes. Every conceivable quirkiness in the mind of man can be found on that strip of paper on chrome.

As to the reasons people attach those sticky banners to their cars, trucks and RVs, some could be:

· Bumper stickers advertise opinions, such as political ones, without your actually having to debate, confront or defend those obviously obtuse ideas you have or that idiot you proclaim has your vote.

· You can be seen as a really humorous person in easy-to-read print – not an easy thing – even though somebody else said it first.

· Your readers will be forced to pronounce bad words when they see your bumper – more perverse humor there.

· Bumper stickers are sometimes free. Like now would be a good time to pick up a supply of Gore stickers.

· People who travel in motor homes like to decorate their

vehicles with tourist decals to show they've "been there, done that."

Large, flat-sided travel vehicles are like great big moving bill boards on which to display your sticker stuff:

"Bridal Veil Falls – See it or be sorry."

"Alexander's Snake and Alligator Farm – Live! Live!"

"I Followed the Crowd to BB's Bar-B-Q."

"The Round Top Fair – Anteeks & Junque."

I also like the one, usually seen stuck to the back window of a pickup truck, prominent but not covering the gunrack, which proclaims philosophically, ---- Happens. Even better is when the ---- is in Spanish.

A few more of my favorite communiqués de bumper collected over the years by my crack staff of collector persons:

· My Kid Beat Up Your Honor Student. What do you suppose possesses a person to stick that in their back window and park at the post office so the whole town can read it?

· "Give Me Ambiguity or Give Me Something Else." What a hoot!

· "Here's to Your Ability to Take Your Virility into Your Senility." Oh, man we hope!

· "What's Another Word for Thesaurus?" On the bumper of an old Volkswagen bus.

· "If You Ain't the Lead Dog, the View Never Changes." 'Nuff said.

· "I'd Give My Right Arm to be Ambidextrous." Another VW – a bug this time.

· "Eschew Obfuscation." This one was printed in odd, clashing colors with kind of scribbled lettering.

And lastly, as well as leastly, two all-time favorite stickers for the bumper:

"Real Men Don't Bond" and

"When They Left Amarillo, Did Anyone Turn Out the Lights?"

One more? Please? Before I see if peanut butter really works to remove sticky from chrome?

"Time Flies Like an Arrow, But Fruit Flies Like a Banana."

Some Mighty Big Numbers

Whatever meager math skills I used to claim have diminished significantly in the last few decades, along with memory skills – if I ever had any.

As the trail of fallen brain cells lengthens while I hobble along, other less mentionable talents have all but disappeared from my arsenal of personal tools for living. Ah-h-h, well . . .

But, I have made a last ditch effort to display some mathematical prowess and, with the help of my trusty little calculator, I have come up with the following absolutely mind-boggling numbers, none of which, aside from boggling a mind or two, are of any practical use whatsoever. But, they were fun to contemplate momentarily. And they will serve as this week's Moment of Silliness.

(We sometimes forget to mention the weekly "moment" in the column, but we want to assume y'all are enjoying a regular silly moment on your own.)

Okay, now for some really big numbers:

How many heartbeats can you count on having if you live to a ripe old 72 like I have? Let's see, take your average heart rate of, say, 60 beats per minute, multiply that by the number of minutes in a day, 720, and you get 43,200 beats per day. Take that already impressive number and multiply it by 365 days and you get

15,768,000 beats per year – that's almost 16 million! In just one year!

Now let's multiply that even more impressive number by 72 and we get, let's see here, could that be right – 1,135,296,000,000? That's one trillion, 135 billion, 296 million!

That is such a humongous number, I feel the need for a long nap. I'm very tired, just thinking about all those thump-thumps.

Whew. You could do the same kind of math in figuring the number of breaths taken in 72 years or the gallons of sweat and tears, if you only had the math skills and energy.

Maybe you're not curious or, worse, maybe you actually have something productive to do with your time. Not to worry – we Different Stuffers are on top of it.

And there's more:

Members of the human race, being what it is, divided into two major groups – your girls and your guys – spend a huge amount of time thinking about the group they're not part of – girls think about guys, guys think about girls.

Okay, here's the question: how many times per waking moment – we won't attempt to count dreams – does this happen? The crack staff of Different Stuff researchers, always on the cutting edge of statistical, demographic research, has the answer to this pressing question.

Leaving out the actual reason the sexes think about each other and taking into account the various ages and other appropriate factors affecting the participants, we can, without reservation, report that the number of times, per waking moment given over to thinking of teenage girls by teenage boys is astronomical. Beyond astronomical, even into infinity.

We can report as well, equally without reservation, almost the same statistical evidence in the reverse case.

The numbers do diminish with the advancing ages of homo sapiens, along with changing reasons girls think of guys. As for the reverse, we don't think the reasons ever change, though the number per waking moment may decrease slightly with antiquity.

Uncle Willie on #Fixin "What Ain't Broke"

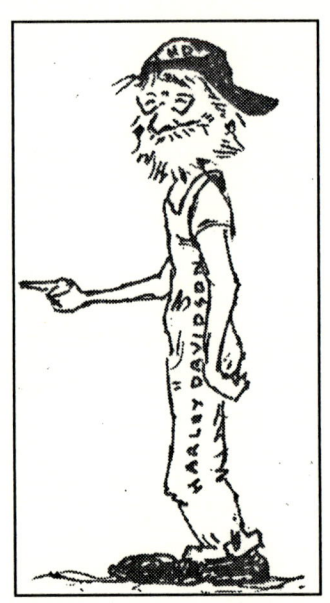

Well, son, I reckon they've gone and did it again, them pesky politicians and government employees. Them folks has decided to spend several million dollars of hard-earned taxpayer dollars to temporarily fix up a problem that don't need to be fixed up. This ain't nothin' new, of course, they's always a-doin' such.

Let me ask you, Billy, did any of them bureaucrats poll you or anybody you know afore they decided to fix up somethin' that don't need fixin'?

Ain't that the way it always is? Nobody ever asks us what we think about what they're a-doin', do they?

But, oncet again, with the help of all them crack researchers you got over there at Different Stuff, I'm ready to leap into the breech just like afore and give them old boys another opinion about what they propose to do by way of fixin' what ain't broke.

I was a-readin' the front page of your paper and the item that caught my attention was the one sayin' that Boerne is ready to "unkink Herff-Esser." The city officials in charge of makin' pronouncements pronounced that the Herff-Esser intersections at Hwy. 46 are ready to be "improved."

Didn't they just get through "improvin'" that there Herff intersection? Yes, they did, costin' umpty-ump thousands of dollars and an interminable stretch of time. We all heaved a sigh of relief and sent thanks to the road gods when it was finally finished. We have certainly been enjoyin' the use of it. Comin' up Herff and gittin' onto Hwy. 46 is real easy now and smooth – a whole lot better'n the old "sheepdip Crossing" was, I'll tell ya.

So, ya have to wait a little bit sometimes to make a left onto Esser Road. What's the big problem? That there is whatcha call a "moot question," Billy. Like a lawyer, I already know the answer to it afore I asked.

The problem is some little high school kids commenced complainin' about having to wait there sometimes up to a minute to hook a left onto Esser so's they can go on down aways there and park on the street – both sides – and have to walk a half-mile to school.

Ain't that a durn shame, Billy? Them kids have to wait a whole minute sometimes to get across from Herff to Esser. So you can figger what happened next, can't ya, son?

Some of them daddies and mommies put a bug in the ear of some of them city officials who announce stuff and the rest is extremely costly history.

You ain't asked fer it either, Billy, but here's what my opinion is anyway. I think it's a good thing to make people wait a minute to get a left turn off a busy highway. They could have a "moment of silence," maybe, where they could think about their drivin' and how lucky they are to even have such a problem.

Slow 'em down, I say. The more times while they're in cars, talkin' on them cell phones, the better. Makin' the traffic move faster ain't a good thing, says I, not always.

Well, there you are Billy, just another half-baked idea from your old Uncle Willie.

PS Just to give 'em their due, them old boys down there at City Hall, the new curb and pavement on Bandera there by the Wal-

Mart is a good thing.

So, ever idea they come up with ain't necessarily a bad one. They'd get even more points, wouldn't they, if they'd come up with a plan to spend that Esser-Herff money on a truck by-pass to get them 18-wheelers offa Main Street.

Stuff d Da Week

Let's begin this week's silliness with some really weird and unusually stupid headlines from various printed publications – newspapers, magazines, periodicals, etc.

They have been gleaned by my crack staff of researchers humped over their computers, whining about wanting overtime, but not about to get any.

These bits of story headlines tend to preclude any desire to read the actual story – it might make some sense, and, as you know, the crack researchers really don't care about making sense. Just having some fun:

· "Police Begin Campaign to Run Down Jaywalkers" competes with "Drunk Gets Nine Months in Violin Case" as the top stupid headline of the week.

· But, wait! How about "Panda Mating Fails; Veterinarian Takes Over." Or, "Typhoon Rips Through Cemetery; Hundreds Dead."

· This recent tabloid - like headline recounts an unfortunate experience in a store which obviously has been extremely short of checkers – "Two Sisters Reunited After 18 Years in Checkout Counter."

Poor things. You can sympathize, can't you.

Picture of the Week. That wonderful, euphoric moment of ecstatic celebration caught by the television cameras last weekend as the Detroit Red Wings hockey team wrapped up the world championship (I guess.)

The film showed one of the players hoisting the trophy over his head while he was being carried around the rink by his teammates
The poor guy had this huge, gap-toothed grin on his face – for real, a couple of front teeth missing. Appropriate, don't
you think, hockey being the rough-and-stumble activity that it is.

Those characters delight in whacking each other with their sticks and pucks and whatever else they can get their hands on.

· Attitude of the Week: This does not refer to the dictionary definition of "attitude," but, rather to the new 90s kind of attitude – aggressive, self-aggrandizing, superiority-establishing, snotty kind of attitude that is so admired by us citizens of the millennium. The competitive, winning-is-everything, losing-is-for-losers attitude.
I saw this on television – a sound-bite, I suppose – and it showed everybody's new hero, Tiger Woods, giving a bad name to the ancient and gentlemanly game of golf by doing an exaggerated hand pump after making a shot.

Oh, I know, it's a common sight – athletes of all stripes do it, but where did our good manners and sense of sportsmanship go? They're lost, aren't they?

Now when we win, we do our best to humiliate the loser because that's what he is, isn't he, a loser! Don't let him forget it! Rub it in! Kick him while he's down!

· Silly Vehicle of the Week. The Land Rover. Unless you actually plan to drive into four feet of water with your kids in the back . . .
Wait a minute! It could be just the car for those numb brains down there in the big city who can't wait for big rains and floods so they can try the low water crossings, giving the police and fire departments a fit.

· One More – Wisdom of the Week. If you don't take care of yourself when you're young, you might not live to regret it.
Truer words weren't ever spake . . .

News From Raelian Land

As one of our infamous "New Year's Resolutions," Different Stuff had promised – just last week – to remain alert for, report on and do all the Silly Moments that come across our desk. Well, we have – as the first shot out of the bag – a truly Silly Moment to report to you. Will miracles never cease?

You readers must be aware of the first bit of New Year's silliness; it's been all over the news. The Talking Heads are beside themselves with glee – all they can do with this is have fun with it.

Cloning!

Yes! It's in the headlines again. But, wait! This time with a weird new twist. This time we're not talking sheep or cows or even rats. This time we're talking alien-built humans. We're beside ourselves, too, on this one and – hold it – we could literally be beside ourselves here.

The phrase takes on a whole new meaning – think about it. "Beside ourselves."

According to the spokesman, Rael, that is, of the Raelians (he would be Headraelian, wouldn't he?), we humans are the result of 25,000 years of DNA experiments by extraterrestrials. We were created in the likeness of them, then transplanted on this up-to-then empty planet.

We were punished for our evil ways with the Great Flood, the

Earth was repopulated with the contents of the ark, which was not all animals "two by two" as we've always heard, but which actually contained DNA from the alien guys and our planet was repopulated with that.

Great story, huh? But, wait, again! The tale is not that far off, is it? Except that the Raelians have no actual God; their explanation – if you can just not get serious for a moment – covers the bases for some folks. It's claimed membership in this weirdness is 55,000 humans in 84 countries.

But now for the Really Silly Part.

Everybody on all sides of the issue is uptight over the whole cloning thing: the Religious Right (who thrive on being Right) think there ought to be a law against it; the Liberal Left (who also love being correct) don't want laws against anything; and the vast crowd of the unwashed Middle-of-the-Roaders (who assume they will never be right) haven't a clue how they feel until Oprah TELLS 'em how they feel.

So, 55,000 fringe element folks may not seem like a lot, but wait! The "squeaky wheel" is squeaking and may have to be greased by all those pesky scientists and bioethicists. Ms. Dr. Brigette, the Chief Scientific Explainer for the Raelans, is certainly garnering more than her allotted 15 minutes of fame, we're here to tell ya.

So, as is our solution to many, many, of our planet's many, many, Silly Moments, we have once again awakened our cousin Goober – thrice removed – and apprised him of the situation.

After he had cleared away some of the cobwebs, we recorded – for the edification of the world – the Goobster's take on the whole thing via his favorite literary vehicle, the limerick.

"Some aliens from way out in space
Invented the whole human race;
They saw us as needing a DNA seeding
So that all could have the same face."

We ourselves are grateful to be able to begin this brand new year with this piece of silliness – it bodes well as the beginning of this year's Silly Moment collection, and it may be hard to top.

The Geezer Perspective

Even old geezers such as me like Michael Jordan.

If you are like me, in fact, you are a basketball fan. I like the game to play it – then – and to watch it – now. From the little kids to the professionals, basketball is a "fan" game – anybody can understand it. You're close to the game physically, it's intimate and understandable.

There is a universal consensus with which I agree – Michael Jordan is the best basketball player in the history of the game. He's everybody's hero, known throughout the world as a champion and as a salesman.

Now, here comes the "Geezer Perspective." As great as he is and as much as I admire all his skills as a player and even his presentability as a TV huckster – heck, I like watching his commercials – geezer that I am, I've never bought a pair of Nikes.

What do you think of that? Young men have been known to rob, cheat, steal, even kill, to put a pair of Nikes on their feet. Young kids beg and plead and whine until their hapless parents give in and get'em some Air Jordans. The durn things aren't cheap, either.

Well, it's a prime example of the good old American Way; that is, the good old American power of advertising and the way we are all influenced by it – nay, DOMINATED by it.

Especially when a celebrity tells us it's just what we need are we controlled by advertising – except if you're a geezer. Then you are "sot in your ways" – that very description you gave to your geezer parents. It's now you. Are you glad? I am.

There is a paucity of benefits accrued by geezers in this life, not a surfeit. There's durn few perks attached to geezerhood, I've noticed.

Maybe a 10 percent discount here and there, free admission to the national parks, your school tax rate is frozen – about time for that one, too, since you haven't had a kid in school in 40 years. You got your Medicare and perhaps a little Social Security check coming in.

Aside from a little break here and there, in fact, it's pretty tough and generally unrewarding, this geezerhood, and not to be undertaken by the trepidatious or the faint of heart.

But, as a veteran geezer myself – one of some experience, getting my time in, so to speak – I'm here to count for you in case you hadn't thought of it yourself, one of the more pleasant, even enriching, perks you should be enjoying as you slip and slide into your dotage.

You do not, repeat, DO NOT, have to buy a pair of Nikes, even though Mr. Michael Jordan implores you to do so.

I do find it's a good feeling to not buy or succumb at all to products hucksdered by famous people. Their entreaties miss the target altogether – I'm sure their feelings might be hurt if they knew.

Know what I think would be a more effective advertising tool!? "Bill Zaner, who's not a celebrity of any sort, wears Nikes and would really like ya'll to buy a pair, too."

Sales to geezers would increase, though some of us would have no need to buy another pair later. But Nike could surely employ another plain, everyday geezer to hustle their shoes.

We'd work much cheaper, too.

Ready - set - obfuscate!

Dr. Language Guy has once again stepped up to the podium with what he hopes is a well-prepared and extremely educational lecture on the more obsolete, if obscure, finer points of our current tendency to use our native language to over-explain absolutely everything. He has collected a few sentences meant to clear up and educate. We shall see.

Our resident expert will attempt to enlighten us on the subjects of Art, Politics and Government and perhaps a bit of Philosophy.

Art, at best a nebulous subject, open to myriad explanations, can be covered by quoting some sentences uttered by another nebulous entity – The Art Critic. (Get ready for some really fanciful adjectives now, purposely obfuscatory says Dr. Language Guy, and he's not sure that some of them weren't just made up. We agree.) (Talking about exhibits of Modern Art here)

"...recall the Sfumato-like effects. ."

"...hastily assembled and jejunely jokey ."

".. a more luminous and revelatory phase.."

"...pummeling the viewer with drama .."

"...swelling blue and green quatrefoils.."

"...the fresh rite, the sensation, the facticity ..."

All well and good, dear reader, but if somebody made any of those statements about my work, I'd take 'em to court!

Dr. Language Guy has a freshly made pronouncement from

the very mouth of our very own president which he thinks illustrates very well the age-old tradition of political obfuscation so finely developed by the office holders of our land:

"We are in a dangerous part of this war, and we are sorry that some Americans have been killed, but it's worth it."

We offer no further comment on that one.

Onward into the fog created by well- meaning philosophers, psychologists, psychiatrists and others who wish to explain things to the rest of us. Oh, we need help, all right, no doubt about it, when we seek the "meaning of life".

As Mr. Descartes, the wise old French guy, puts it, "There is nothing so strange and so unbelievable that it has not been said by one philosopher or another."

Before we present what we consider the ultimate philosophically obfuscatory sentence, one which we hated to come to the end of, let us quote but one more well-known philosopher, a Mr. Pascal, who was heard to utter, "Making fun of philosophy is really philosophizing."

Okay, here it is, that incredible sentence, quoted by the Feb. 14, 1983, New Yorker magazine, from "The Context of Self" by Richard M. Zaner:

"To the contrary, precisely because of the contextural (ie, complexural) relatedness among selves, selves are immanently (ie, reflexively) presenced to one another by way of their mutuality, their enabling/enabled relationships – ie, 'spirit' as 'empowering' of self by the other self is the very texture of the 'self-relatedness' of the relation that related itself to its own self and by so relating relates itself to the empowering other self, and of course, conversely."

Richard M. Zaner, or more properly, Dr. Richard M. Zaner, as some of you may know, is my baby brother, the offshoot brother, the one with the huge brain, philosophy is his game.

We've not been keeping score, but we think Dr. Dick is ahead.

(Hint: read that sentence out loud.)

Round File Stuff

It seems an interminable time since we've dumped the wastebasket on the floor and examined the contents therein. Or was it just yesterday?

They say you can tell a lot about folks by performing a postmortem on their trash and, by golly, they may be right.

In the case of our Different Stuff offices, the home base of the Crack Staff of Reporters, there is a veritable mountain of semi-usable detritus. We say "usable" because we once thought it was such. Why else would we have kept it. And kept it. And kept it. And did we use it? No, we did not. But, we must tell about our trash, the better to know us. Ha!

This is that rare description, the one you've always looked for – the triple oxymoron – ready! Luxury Sport Utility. Typical Round File Stuff.

And, for you politically correct fans, the latest, most up-to-date he-she silliness: The US Maritime Commission, in a peculiar attempt to satisfy everybody, has adopted a resolution which will change forever the ages-old tradition of referring to ships as "she." The ship will henceforth be known as "it." Capt. Cook and Magellan, too just rolled over in their watery graves.

A lot of our Round File Stuff is recycled wisdom – you've heard it before. But in case you haven't:

"Love is grand, divorce is a couple-hundred grand."

"Separating the wheat from the chaff." What the heck is

"chaff?" Should it be separated from wheat? Can it be separated? Why? Who cares? I'm just reporting the trash, folks.

Why do gorillas have big nostrils? Because gorillas have big fingers.

"Second hand snuff-dipping is hazardous to your health," a report states, "even if you're friends with a dipper. In order to be a really cool cowboy, though, you do need to own a can to put in the back pocket of your Levi's so you'll have that macho imprint."

We think it's also cool to have acquaintances who do stupid, dangerous things, such as running with the bulls in Pamplona, Spain. Sure, it's only second-hand coolness, but a lot less hazardous.

This is not news, I guess, but we do occasionally miss the old days when there were a lot more good guys, people whose word was bankable, who returned your calls, who really cared how you feel. The perplexing question posed by this old dinosaur, "Why is the proportion of good guys not increasing with the growing population? Just one more rhetorical ..

One for you esoterica aficionados: "the basic struggle of art is to leave out all but the essentials." We already hear some rumblings of disagreement, no doubt from those artists who have a one-hair brush and enormous patience and time on their hands.

One more scrap from the trash can for you country music fans, a couple of song titles: "How Can I Miss You If You Won't Go Away?" and "My Wife Ran Off With My Best Friend and I Sure Do Miss Him."

55 Cancri

Today, we'll display our scientific acumen by discussing some aspects of the science of astronomy and, I suppose, a pinch of astrophysics.

This topic has to do with the recent discovery of another planet in our own Milky Way galaxy which, they tell us, definitely resembles in size and length of orbit around its sun our very own giant planet Jupiter.

Yes, Mr. Big. With the humongous red spot. The planet that takes 15 years to orbit Old Sol!

There is, of course, a sun in this new galaxy named 55 Cancri – I've no idea why that name was chosen, or where the heck numbers 54 or 56 are – that this Jupiter-like planet rotates around.

I guess the astronomer who made this discovery stared into his telescope for the whole 15 years or so of this planet's orbit in order to prove it is, indeed, an orbiter. Your basic astronomer is a very patient man!

So, here's this huge chunk of rock out there doing its thing around its own sun in its own galaxy and, not only that, it is accompanied apparently by a couple of smaller planets which are orbiting much faster and much closer to their sun.

This whole thing of the three planets inhabiting Galaxy 55 Cancri has led some of us more forward thinking wannabe astronomers to conclude – dare we say it – that perhaps there is in the habitable zone between Jupiter's twin and maybe the twin of our planet Venus another, as yet undiscovered, "Third Rock from the Sun."

OK, let us assume for the merest of moments that such is out there, yet unnamed, yet unidentified positively as a parallel universe to our own. I like assumption. There are after all, say those pesky astronomers, a couple hundred billion stars in the Milky Way, most of which we can't even see and therefore cannot prove they don't contain galaxies and planets.

Let us, for a few more mere moments, suspend our regular, everyday, mundane left brains and contemplate this: Out of the 200 billion chances that we know about the infinite universe, a very small drop in a very large bucket, there is one rather obscure, unimpressive little galaxy which is almost the exact mirror image of our sun and our planets.

There is a Mercury, hot and uninhabitable so close to its sun, a wet, warm Venus, and Earth, which we'll come back to. Assume a red Mars and a ringed Saturn. Jupiter we already know. Uranus, distant and cold, and even a Pluto. I know, I forgot one, but did I say almost? Oh, yes – Neptune.

We know this universe. 55 Cancri, is our twin for there we are hurtling about the sun in the same 365 days and having a satellite moon orbiting us every month or so. It's just like Mother Earth and as further proof, we zoom in and observe that our twin planet has all the same peculiarities, some of which we notice right away.

The population of beings scurrying over and above the surface are like so many ants, though not so productive. We recognize ourselves: Republicans and Rappers, Baptists and Britneys, Golfers and Gurus, Sir Micks and SUV drivers.

There's an assortment of other worthies as well, who exhibit human and near-human behavior, such as paying a dollar or more for a pint of tap water somebody put in a plastic bottle with a cute label on it.

We'd be right at home, wouldn't we, on "Third Rock II."

quoting the quaddler

In a recent Sticks and Stones column in the Recorder, Senor Ed Davis claimed he was making room in his allotted space for a "guest columnist" to hold forth on the provided platform. It was not that difficult for him to do so since the invited 'guest' is a most inimitable entity in his own right and we are all aware that in the game of journalism, inimitability is enviable!

His mystery guest columnist presented his thought, I thought, in a most thoughtful and erudite manner. Choosing for his writings subjects of current topical interest to the citizens of our fair township, he took to task some of the prominent, in-the-news politicians and other unpalatables currently bending the simple minds of the voting and the non voting public. The guest is a loveable old quaddler, indeed.

I echo the sentiments of "Uncle Chili" without reservation – he indeed tells it like it is! As a proffered addition to the intimations, innuendos and scurrilous commentary offered up by the mystery guest, let me present a brief, but certainly pungent, couple of paragraphs authored – without editing, by the way – by a cryptic professional journalist of my own acquaintance.

I render the same admonition to my readers: if you're able to guess the identity of my guest ghost, let not a clue slip out...

"I think it must have occurred in ought-six or seven, or it might have been during the Big War – there were two of them, you know – but I must needs ascertain the veritability of my assertions in the following manner. I will question the Chief."

"You're full of it, sir," the Chief alleges, "the story you're attempting to recall never actually occurred at all!"

"But . . " I begin.

"No 'buts' about it," my old ally states, "you're trying to peck out on your old Underwood a soliloquized sequence of events that erupted only last week. Remember now?"

"I am a professional writer, my dear, don't forget capable of entertaining and educating the unwashed masses in an inimitable manner. My Lingua Lexicona is poised, yet readable to the most lackluster of intellects. I am also most capable of presenting in my writings multitudinous, unequivocally precise facts and figures gleaned from my many decades of gleaning things. I have diffused a variety of effluvium into the general body of literature over my span of years as a journalist, memorable for its significance and substantiality. I do not mendaciloquate, though I confess to a lifetime of epistemophilia, the disease of the inveterate lexicographer. Let's just ask my pal Hal, who is always standing by."

"Which Big War was it, old pal Hal?" I queried.

"I have to go along with the Chief on this one," says he, "insofar as the statement about your being 'full of it,' at least. As to which week the story you're attempting to recall for us actually occurred, or if it occurred at all, I cannot verify. My sorrow is without depth, but very sincere."

"It begins to look as though, in my professional journalistic efforts, I may have to resort to a selection of four-letter words. One or two spring immediately to mind – a True Tale will Tell itself, by Heck! But lest I quaddle overmuch, I now desist momentarily."

(My guest columnist has requested I not define every word he writes.)

"No Problem" a Problem

Here we go – more language deficiencies and misusage. Last time I talked about old-fashioned (archaic) words, totally out-of-date verbal communication and why we find it necessary to seek counseling in times of crisis because we simply do not have skills in person-to-person verbal exchange. We lack, sadly, vocabulary and the necessary expertise in its usage.

Dr. Language Guy

I'm in dire personal danger of losing more and more brain cells-in short supply already – as I go about my daily rounds. My chores necessitate verbal exchanges with various people, either in person or electronically.

Those exchanges, in turn, trigger what seems to be the most common response from these various folks when I say, "Thank you."

Please, someone tell me what "no problem" has to do with "thank you?"

It causes brain cell death in my head whenever I hear "no problem" in response to my "thanks."

I know people say that automatically, without thinking, and therein lies the problem – no thinking.

You know you don't really have that person's attention, don't you, when they mechanically reply to your "thanks" with "no problem."

And, I must sadly report, the numbing response is not limited to any specific age group. Alas, you'll hear it from an occasional geezer, too.

What is going on here? This phenomenon has to be closely related to the universal language polluters "you know" and "like."

These brain-numbing speech impediments have probably done more to lower standards of human verbal exchange than any colloquialism in the past 100 years.

It has become "cool" (another one) to converse badly. Or, perhaps, it is "uncool" to speak properly.

Next to the ubiquitous "no problem," the non-thought phrase one hears all too commonly is the cell stupefying "Have a nice day."

Okay, thanks for your good wishes, but are you saying that to me because you sincerely wish for me a nice day, full of fulfilled wishes, a day of comfort, wealth and happiness?

Or, is your so-called brain set on autopilot?

It's not very difficult to find many people of all ages whose speech patterns are that stilted and habitual, who will mutter all of these cliched utterances in their daily chatter.

And to set them off, all you have to say is "thank you."

"Like, no problem" they will respond. "Cool. Have a, like nice day, you know."

Then, like the Different Stuff observer and critic of the Social Condition Prevalent at the Onset of the 21st Century, you can take more or less silent umbrage at such exchanges and make personal vows to do what you can to stem the tide of language decline by never replying to a "thank you" with "no problem." Or "like." Or "you know."

Cool, dude. Okay?

New York - 1; Texas - 0

I've never tried to do it myself, so I can't really say it's not possible. To do what? Talk on a cell phone while simultaneously trying to steer my SUV safely in a traffic situation where lots of other SUVs are whizzing around, some of their drivers trying to avoid hitting me while they, too have this electronic brain cell destroyer stuck to the sides of their heads.

One hopes that their phone conversations are not as important as mine, are inane and unnecessary so that their few remaining brain synapses would be able to zero in on their driving skills, at least enough to prevent their SUV from crashing into mine.

Of course, if in this hypothetical instance my cell phone jabber can't be put off for the minute-and-a-half it would take for me to pull off the road somewhere to use the instrument, then perhaps some of you could see your way to pray for me.

Okay, I realize how much life depends on "keeping in touch," but cell phone addicts, have you ever considered, bad driving habits aside, what life would be like without a cell phone?

You could actually complete a trip to the grocery store without calling home with the question, "Do you want paper or plastic?" (Yes, I actually heard that one!)

You could have a nice, quiet meal in a nice, quiet restaurant without disturbing other dinners with that chirping device you're never without.

A sporting event could be enjoyed start to finish. An intellectual discussion with friends could be savored without intrusion.

Oh, and this one is pretty far out – you could sit on the porch and ponder the universal questions of life, such as, can I survive in a reasonable fashion without my electronic addiction?

Sure, returning to that pesky driving-while-jabbering thing, there are lots of other distractions we are all guilty of engaging in as we drive. You know what they are. Drinking a cup of hot coffee on your way to work or lighting up a smoke – double-whammy there! Both are common distractions from the main business of trying not to commit vehicular manslaughter.

Eating is another. Lots of us munch while driving.

Some of the worst are those who don't allow enough time before getting in the car to finish their grooming. I've seen 'em myself, driving while applying mascara and lipstick, shaving and reading. Wow! That one may be worse than cell phoning.

Now, Texas, second most populous state in the union – meaning we have a huge number of cars and cell phones – is falling dangerously behind in concocting new and sometimes silly and unenforceable legislation meant to protect ourselves from ourselves.

We're really not prepared for which state has beat us to that punch. Can hardly even say it, but, I must. Here goes – the state which has passed a law making it illegal to talk on a hand-held cell phone while committing an act of driving, subject to fines and imprisonment, is, ready? – New York!

Boy, don't that fry yore grits!

(For whatever records that are kept, I have neither an SUV nor a cell phone. But, you probably guessed that already.)

Uncle Willie's Helpful Huntin' Tips

I see by the paper that them eager beaver "hunters" is out there knockin' each other off again this year.

I put them quotation marks around the word "hunter" because there ain't a real "hunter" in the bunch. They're just amateurs, after all. They don't hunt much fer a livin', do they? Or even for food, though they probably do eat the deer meat to justify the trouble and expense they go to to get it. Or, what's worse, they'll give it to some of us "non-hunters" who they know would never eat anything with eyes like that.

Anyways, there they are trompin' around there in the brush with their silly camouflage suits on, like them deer can't see 'em makin' noise, flippin' beer cans all over the place, just generally actin' weird. And pretty stupid too.

So, even if they don't deserve any help, I've decided to give a few hints so's that maybe they'll stop plugging each other with their guns.

Hint number one: Sell all your guns. Even at a pawn shop, you can git a good price.

Hint number two: With yer gun and bullet money, buy yourself a good camera.

Hint three: Take some lessons in photographing Bambi's and wild turkeys and little doves and bunnies and wild pigs and mountain lions and bears and stuff.

Hint four: To keep things even, keep your camouflage suit, but drink beer out of returnable bottles.

Hint five: Take your wives and kids out there with you. You know you don't act stupid when they're with you.

Now, I know you old boys think that huntin's a real "man" thing to do, very "macho" and all, and that there's way too many of them pesky deer and turkeys and everything. You're only helpin' out the environment if you slay a few of 'em and throw 'em over the hood of yer car and drive around like that with yer arm out the window and yer camouflage hat pushed back real proud.

But, maybe ya'll could just get together in one of your garages, wear your suits, play some cards, drink some beer, and tell lies to each other about yer former exploits about the ones that got away. Then go in the house and admire yer deer photos.

Oh, nephew Goober has wrote one of them "limericks" fer you "hunters" and asked me to put it in this here column.

> *The 'hunters' were out with their guns,*
> *They'd shoot at what flies or what runs,*
> *So, in their great haste*
> *With bullets to waste,*
> *They shot Uncle George in the buns."*

That Goober, he's somethin', ain't he?

Mysteries Explained (Finally)

This is definitely wide-open territory. There are more than a few myths and mysteries out there in that jungle – myths and mysteries which beg to be explained, to be "de-mysteried."

And who better to do that than your intrepid reporter here, with the help, of course, of my crack staff of investigative researchers, those researchers being totally dedicated to researching whatever I tell them needs researching.

Mystery One:

Why don't you get all the romance you want – why is your love life something less than you could reasonably expect? You're a nice person with fairly good personal hygiene. You're not offensive in your appearance or your social graces. You have at least some financial security, and you dress well.

So how come you don't have a crowd of opposite sex members lined up to kiss you?

Well, I and my crack staff have the answer. You ready? Your lips are too thin. They have not been enhanced, silicon-wise. Yes, it's true. Nobody wants to kiss people with thin lips. Everybody wants to kiss people with swollen, fat, juicy-looking lips.

Sad but true.

Mystery Two:

Why are you not as influential as you'd like to be? Why do

you have difficulty getting people to bend to your will? Why do people ignore you when you attempt to dominate a conversation? You are a reasonably intelligent and mature individual with lots of good ideas, and you feel you have many positive contributions to make which would insure a better quality of life for all the citizens of the world. But all those citizens merely look right through you, or past you, or worse, over your head!

Again, I and my crack staff have researched this unfortunate situation and have, again, come up with a de-mystification: you are too short.

That's right, you are not tall enough; you are altitudinally challenged; you have runt genes.

Our research indicates that everybody listens to tall people, even if they are dumb as a handful of gravel. Nobody looks through, past or over a tall person. Tall people are allowed to dominate, bend and contribute. For example, could you prevent David Robinson from dunking? You could not.

Mystery Three:

Why don't you have all the money you want? You are fairly comfortable, you think; but you could sure use a little more, couldn't you? You feel you have worked hard, been diligent with your investments and your disposable income, you've done without some new SUVs and big screen TVs. You're a real striver and have not been afraid to jump right in when a financial opportunity presented itself.

So how come you always run out of money before you run out of bills? Why aren't there more zeros behind your income numbers?

Yes, indeed, we've demysteried this mystery: you are too short, and you have thin lips! Both! Too many strikes – nobody wants to kiss you, and everybody looks right over you.

For more de-mystification, stay tuned to future columns.

Save Any Time Lately?

Do you drive just little bit over the speed limit on the way to work to save a few seconds?

Did you combine your errands into one trip so you'll save some time?

How about laying out things you're going to wear tomorrow the night before and setting the coffee maker so you can sleep in an extra few minutes?

Did you have a convenient, nourishing breakfast bar this morning instead of actually fixing a real breakfast? Time saved there, you know.

Did you get fed news updates electronically rather than sitting down and reading the paper? Add another few seconds saved.

E-mail your friends instead of writing an old-fashioned, time-consuming letter? Saved a bunch of minutes there, you can bet.

And the e-mail recipient saves time, too, not having to waste precious seconds opening that foolish envelope. You both get ahead in time-saving effort by e-mailing.

Anyway, these are a few examples of things you might have done to save time. I'm confident you have many more time-saving devices, ploys or short-cuts.

So, this very column you're wasting valuable seconds reading appears in your very own Hill Country Recorder under the title, "Leisure Time." Is there a message there?

The other question becomes then, not so much "have you saved any time lately," but rather, "what did you do with it?"

Did you do "Leisure" with any of it? And just what the heck is "leisure," anyway?

So many up-to-date type people seem to equate leisure with sweating while doing some strenuous sports activity that requires lots of energy and money – hang-gliding, snow-boarding, doing the triathlon, rowing a boat around the world or climbing Mt. Everest.

Wow! Are you saving up your time so you can do that kind of stuff?

Well, then what? Why don't we see if we can think up some useful ways to use that 12 seconds you saved this morning while you ate, shaved, put on your makeup, talked on your cell phone and finished getting dressed while you drove a little too fast going to work.

Use two of those valuable seconds giving your wife or husband an extra hug.

Two more ticks of the old clock could be devoted to establishing a more meaningful bond with your kids.

Maybe three seconds could be spent in profound contemplation of the meaning of life.

One big second to solving the national debt.

For the last four, let's activate, if we can, a few of our atrophied brain cells and let Cousin Goober compose a poem with a complex explanation of the mysteries and problems inherent in this busy, fast-paced world.
Like:

> *The ants in their nest how they fled*
> *Around and around,*
> *How they sped,*
> *Their duties were varied, that's why they were harried –*
> *They fled and they sped, and then they were dead.*

Okay, I confess it took him five seconds to compose that poem. The national debt will have to wait until tomorrow.

From Whence Came We?

It's a good question. Asked by every human being who's ever lived, I suspect – philosophers, thinkers, gurus and just plain people whose minds have occasionally gotten off the mundane and drifted into deeper waters. That's it – waters. Being in or next to water seems to cause folks to want to meditate – to ponder the more profound aspects of their existence.

As I did on my last visit to the coast. I found myself musing on the metaphysics of the human situation as I watched the hypnotic movement of the waves rolling in gently to shore.

The Question once again came into my mind: Which? Evolution or Creation? regarding the How of human existence. The Why is probably unanswerable, by me anyway.

The biggest part of any human being is his EGO. We all regard ourselves as really important in the Grand Scheme, so we love to give ourselves the advantage, rate ourselves number one overall. Never mind the bugs and birds and bears.

Anyway, as a novice, largely unpracticed thinker, I hereby set forth on these uncharted waters with these thoughts:

Evolution. Did we human beings begin our journey in the Pelagic ooze, filtering nourishment for our one-celled bodies from that sea and slowly squirm onto dry land, gradually metamorphosing into various kinds of scaly reptiles?

Did we next, over millions of years, evolve into hair-covered, knuckle-dragging simian creatures, grunting and howling at one another from our perches in the trees, and drop to the ground to stand upright on our hind legs, as our brains slowly increased in size, if not usefulness? Did we slog torturously through recent millennia to our present state of being suburban homeowners, fussing, fighting, forming into bands of Democrats and Republicans who sit on the couch and watch football on weekends?

And Creation. Did we human beings materialize suddenly, as from a magician's puff of smoke into our present two-legged form, hairless bodies gleaming and big brains humming with fully formed abstract thoughts?

Were other-colored humans, like brown ones, black ones, red and yellow ones included in that original production? Have we proceeded agonizingly, with much suffering and abuse, through these recent thousands of years, fussing and fighting and grunting and howling at one another, asserting our superiority over those whose brains seem not to be as large as our own?

Did we come to our present level of civilized behavior in which we've formed ourselves into religious and political bands of our own exact kind so we can go to church on Sundays, vote once every four years, and raise cain in between times?

Well, as you can plainly see, I haven't answered anything. I've only asked more questions, and the whole thing has given me a headache. Therefore, I'll save the other big Question, "To Whence Go We?" for a future column – maybe pondered and written from that other good thinking place – a mountaintop.

Different Wise Stuff

I think it is a worthy ambition to work toward becoming a wise old person, one who has learned enough about the vagaries of life as we know it to be able to come up with an appropriate profundity to which younger, not-so-wise beings will take heed.

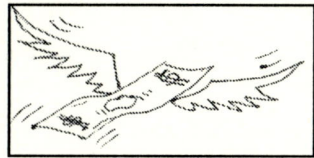

Unfortunately for the younger beings who are within my sphere of influence, I am not a wise old person, but merely an old person.

"Age doesn't always bring wisdom – sometimes it comes alone."

Now whoever it was who first said that was a wise old coot.

It's most distressing to think that sometime along my torturous and convoluted path of existence, I actually may have had a wise thought, but failed to write it down. The truly prudent sage takes notes, I prudently note.

I do have theories, though, many of them half-baked and others not baked at all. One holds that the human brain can contain only a certain amount of information. We do not lose our memories as much as is claimed. I think our brainpans merely fill up and are unable to accept new intelligence.

However, should a new bit of knowledge somehow penetrate, an old piece of data must be vacated to make room. You can actually see these bits of old stuff flaking off people like so much dandruff.

Flaking dandruff aside, there have gone before us many wise old coots who had many wise things to pass on to any younger beings willing to listen. That, perhaps, could be one of the beginning signals of oncoming wisdom – willingness to listen.

"If'n you ain't listen', you ain't learnin'!" is a wisdom attributed to Elvis Presley, of all people. Just give the quote a moment.

There is a ray of hope in listening to some acknowledged wise old coots such as some of the old Greeks. Aristotle, for example, said "Knowing what is right does not make a sagacious man."

And what striving wise person among us could disagree with Voltaire – "The more I read, the more I meditate; and the more I acquire, the more certain I am that I know nothing."

Or "If a little knowledge is dangerous, where is the man who has so much as to be out of danger?" This last is accredited to a wise old geezer named TH Huxley.

The ancient Chinese philosophers were no pikers, either, when it came to dispensing sagacity. "The beginning of wisdom is to call things by their right names," said one.

Among my favorite wise old guys are a couple of more modern coots who had a way of dispensing a lot of wisdom in the form of tiny, pungently phrased poems.

First a fellow named Piet Hein who penned this jewel:
"The road to wisdom:
Well, it's plain and simple to express:

> Err
> And err
> And err again,
> But less
> And less
> And less."

And a gem by Ogden Nash:
> "That money talks, I'll not deny
> When it talks to me, it says 'Good-bye.'"

Games We Used to Play

Here comes another of those infamous Different Stuff nostalgia columns. We've assigned our crack research staff to do what it does peerlessly – research the obscure. It seems that people are not as creative as they used to be. Oh, we know, look at all the "technical" knowledge so many of us possess. Lots of us can program a VCR or do brain surgery.

We can, even as children, figure out how to win a video game. We possess more information per square millimeter of gray matter than we ever have.

In short, we are able to avail ourselves of an entire universe of stuff which can inform and entertain us endlessly. And many of us are, indeed, informed, to the point of overload. And we are in constant pursuit of pleasure and entertainment, although there's not much pursuit to it. It's all easily available and simply provided. In fact, often it's the entertainment that does the pursuing.

But we Different Stuffers ask, "Can we use our brains to invent or imagine or create?"

Our kids don't seem to be able to play without parental organization. Do you ever see a kid today making up a game?

Way back in the Paleolithic era, when present day geezers were kids, games were invented. Did you ever make a functional, locomoting vehicle out of a thread spool, piece of soap and a rubber band, for example? How about a really fast, leg-powered scooter out of one old roller skate, a couple of two-by-fours and, if you wanted a fancy one, an old apple crate? How many kids today would even know what a thread spool, four-wheel roller skate or an apple crate is?

Could one of today's kids climb a tree and just sit there for hours, perhaps imagining he could fly? Or lie on his back in the grass and make stuff out of passing clouds? Or build an entire city on a dirt pile, complete with buildings and streets and parks?

Here's a good one this old geezer and his brother and friends used to do almost every Saturday morning in those lovely, bygone summers – which lasted an endless, full three months, by the way.

We'd take our 11 cents saved up during the week and take in the regular Saturday morning "serial" at the movie theatre.

There, in the bedlam of the darkened room, we'd watch the weekly episode of the big western stars of the day – Roy Rogers, Hopalong Cassidy, Gene Autry the Singing Cowboy, et al.

The great part of this routine occurred when we went home. There, after much very loud wrangling and discussion, we'd choose our parts and relive the entire episode we'd just seen. Our roles were never the same, I remember. I'd be Roy one week and a Black Hat the next. I did get to play Gabby Hayes a lot, though - perhaps an omen.

"Bang, you're dead!"

"Naw, you missed!"

"Pow! Roy never misses!"

We could recreate sound effects perfectly – at least to our ears – gunshots, different, of course, from rifle shots, galloping, as opposed to walking horses, Indian yells, arrows striking their targets – "shhhhh-thunk!" Even some of the background orchestral accompaniment.

Boy, that was fun! I sort of feel sorry for a kid who's never had a chance to be Roy Rogers. Or Gabby Hayes, the first sidekick.

I can still do Gabby by the way, and now I look the part.

The Lady Sings Fat

Obsessed with your weight? Hate your body? Think Calista Flockhart possesses the ideal figure? Love to eat?

Well, we assigned our crack Different Stuff research staff to delve into the modern obsession with excess avoirdupois.

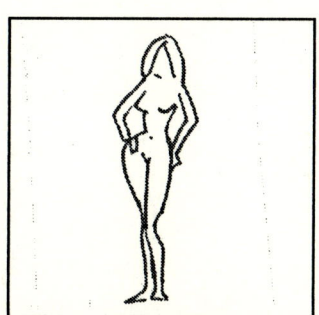

Their diligent delving has resulted in just one important conclusion – designers of clothing are the only people who like skinny men and women. That's it.

Nobody in the general population, least of all guys, likes skinny women. Ask us. We'll tell you we prefer a little meat on the bones.

I, of course, guy that I am, can only be a spokesman for the guy population, and I think after all these many decades of close and astute observations of the female segment, really skinny women are not appealing to us guys, no matter how attractive they might look in their designer togs.

Curves! That's what we want! Soft curves, not hard, bony angles. C'mon, ladies. You know a lot of what you do is for the benefit of a guy – boyfriend, husband or prospective boyfriend or husband.

Conversely, nearly everything we do is for the benefit and pleasure of our girlfriend, wife or mother.

Such is the way of humankind, reports the staff who have been seriously researching new ways to eliminate stress from our lives.

Among other conclusions, they have determined that if we

could all adopt their new philosophy of well being, that "fat is where it's at," much of the stress of daily living could be eliminated.

With the introduction of their new American Philosophy of Phat," the staff has once again endeavored to awaken our Cousin Goober and entreat him to limerickally express the tried and true ideology first expressed many years ago by Alfred E. Newman, the Phirst Phriend of the Phatties and Phounder of the Phat Philosophy.

Goober, after much grumbling about being awakened from his day long nap, has complied with the following:

> *There was a Fat Lady who sang it*
> *Whenever the show ended, said 'dang it.'*
> *It's really okay*
> *Not to care what you weigh,*
> *And let all the skinnies go hang it.*

We believe Goober has nailed it with this bit of doggerel – and we will continue to expound the stress-reducing benefits of the Phat Philosophy.

While it is true that guys aspire to large, muscular physiques for themselves, they attest to a preference for naturally curvy women – soft and feminine are the key words there – and we think that the supermodel with the broomstick figure would never be asked, as is the Fat Lady, to sing.

Imagine – "It ain't over 'til the Skinny Lady sings."

Ain't never gonna happen.

Doctor Language Guy

I was hoping this new and untested millennium would bring about an enlightened awareness of proper language usage by the American masses. Apparently I was too optimistic in wishing for improved syntax and hyperbole, or at least premature in that regard.

Dr. Language Guy

The careful speaker, the sensitive writer of our common language appears to be, like other aspects of life in the last century, less influential than ever.

Orators and writers had a profound effect on their audiences throughout most of the history of our country and people listened and read and cared about communicating with words written in beautiful, poetic ways.

I'm not talking about the flowery speech of the days of Shakespeare or William Jennings Bryan, but ordinary proper usage, spelling and pronunciation. It would be nice, for instance, to hear an adult speak just once without degenerating into the vernacular of teenagers.

Kids have their own colloquial way of speaking and I, for one, won't get into it with them. It is impossible for me to intersperse the word "like" into my conversations at all, much less four or five times per sentence. Nor can I see the sense of using "goes" for "says."

Examples of speech of persons who put absolutely no thought into their conversation:

No. 1 – "I, like, saw Kimberly, and she goes, like, you know, where've you been?"
No. 2 – "I have to, like, go?"
No. 3 – "He goes, like, my tires cost, like, $1,200 apiece?"
No. 4 – "Don't, like, go out with him. He, like, goes, you know, like, I have to, like, borrow my dad's car?"

Oh, yes. Let me mention the universal tendency to end every statement on an upward note, as though it were a question requiring acknowledgement. I suppose it's because of the speaker's need to be recognized.

As in, "I, like, heard him say, like, I have a doctor's appointment today?" No period.

Isn't proper language usage being taught in our schools anymore? Do the teachers themselves speak this way? Are students required to actually compose coherent sentences and paragraphs? What happened to our traditions of oral and written communication?

I hope that things will get better, that people will begin to care again about our language and find in it the beauty I always have.

My dear mother instilled the love of reading and writing in me and my brother when we were kids and though I'm sure we probably veered off course during our teen years, we both are back. We both read and we both write and we both appreciate and nuture our basic means of communication.

Footnote: Mr. Language Guy is still hearing "Realtor" pronounced "Real-a-tor" and thinks, with all those in Boerne engaged in that occupation, that, hey, we could pronounce our own job right, at least!

Like, hey, you know, like, I go, I like, hey, you know, like.

There! I don't have to use that stuff now for several more sentences.

Artstuff

It goes without saying – but I'm going to say it anyway – that I do a lot of thinking aboutthe subject of art.

That is not to say that I've got anything actually figured out, though. Far from that, I may have come to even fewer conclusions here in my "autumn years." Fewer conclusions, in fact, about everything.

But, I still think about art quite a bit of the time, such as at 3 am when I'll sit bolt upright, as goes the idiom, with some astounding revelation on the subject.

"Eureka!" I'll cry, "the final answer is."

You other geezers out there will be able to empathize with this kind of thing. Next morning, if you can remember at all, your astounding revelation will not astound in the bright light of day.

I've heard people say of thoughts in the night that they'll immediately take action, such as writing it down or even making a sketch if it's some solution to an artwork they have in progress.

I myself have done neither of those things, being mostly anxious to get back to sleep, for cryin' out loud.

In a broad sense – leaving plenty of wiggle room – it could be said that art is my life, or even that life is my art, though the latter statement would require somewhat deeper thought than I've given it so far.

I do hear other artists talk about their art and their lives, though.

A brief pause here to say that one conclusion I can assert with some degree of finality is that most of the artists I've known do relish any discussion about themselves and their art. They do, in fact, panic if more than a few minutes are spent on another subject.

They apparently have no answers either, other than to talk about it. Maybe an open-ended discussion of the aspects of Life as Art or Art as Life is enough. Talking about it without arriving at conclusions is what we do anyway. Philosophizing is Phun!

I'll take another random direction on the subject. This has to do with what I hear from people in general.

"My mother paints" or "I have a son who's real interested in art" or even "I've always wanted to try it, but never had the time."

My comment to these statements more often than not – and you know my comments are worth exactly what you paid for them – is "artists are born, I think."

If a person – big "if," is an artist, one who does art most of the time and thinks about art when he's not doing it, that person was born an artist.

Artists are not made or taught. Artists just are. Even if you've never done any art, I believe that if you think about it lots of your conscious time, and maybe you never create anything with physical form to it, you're thinking like an artist so you are one. How 'bout that!

I suspect there are many, many people out there who think as an artist does and, therefore, can lay claim to the title.

On the other hand, there are lots of folks who own a paintbrush who should trade it in on a golf club and enjoy art from a distance.

RX: A Moment of Silliness

Different Stuff's crack researchers have held a lifelong belief that what makes life worthwhile is the enjoyment, every now and then, of a Moment of Silliness, a snippet of time, a split second even, wherein mundanity is momentarily suspended and routine and serious thought is abandoned–just for a moment.

Something sort of snaps in your head, and you feel instantaneously giddy. You want to smile, maybe even burst out laughing. You've seen or thought of something totally ludicrous, so out of sync with present goings-on-like a complete non sequitur – you can't help yourself. It's just too silly.

"Lighten up!" is a well-used expression, usually spoken by people who believe you're in a state of distress. But that's not what we're talking about here. No, we're talking about the everyday job of living – you know, where you get into this rut and your brain slips into neutral and you just glide along. Nothing really wrong with getting into that mode, we guess – it's just not a very exciting or interesting way to pass your days.

Our crack staff has decided that we all need that wonderful Moment of Silliness, not every now and then but every day.

How can we do this? Until you become proficient at locating and appreciating Silly Stuff, we can offer the help you need. Go to the silly doctor and get a prescription.

Don't know a silly doctor? Okay. In the interim, let us call upon the silliest person we know, our slow-witted but extremely nonsensical cousin Goober, to compose an appropriate limerick:

The best way to really be silly
Is to think of what-ifs like ol' Billy
It's always a hoot to give good sense the boot,
And foment a moment that's silly.

Forgive him; he hasn't brushed all the cobwebs out of his so-called brain like we told him to.

We believe that a daily shot of Vitamin S is essential for our good health. Without it, we're liable to contract that most dreaded of human ailments, boredom.

Look around you. You can usually pick out the people who've had their dose of silly for the day. Look in their eyes – there's just a hint of a giggle just past or on the way. They've had a moment. They've thought of something ludicrous – a "what if."

Maybe they saw these headlines that we noted:

"Two sisters reunited after 18 years in checkout counter."

"Cold wave linked to temperatures."

"New study of obesity looks for larger test group."

Yes, research by our crack staff proves that people who receive a daily dose of Vitamin S, which results 100 percent of the time in a Moment of Silliness, live longer and better.

There's a world of what-ifs to enjoy, so go on out there and quit thinking. Have a moment of absurdity. You'll be glad you did.

LC The Cat's Pet Man

"There I was, minding my own cat-business on the shore of Boerne Lake where I'd been dumped. I was doing okay, scrounging a living as only a kitty can do, mooching or swiping food as I had to, snagging an occasional bug or moth or perhaps a yummy rodent. Then, as only Fate can have it, there appeared right there in my territory, the Man. My Man!

"I knew. It was love at first sight. He was an old geezer, bandy-legged in his cut-offs standing there watching his grandkids cavorting in the water.

"Ever so slyly, in my time-honored cat way, I slinked up to him and wound my lithe young body sinuously around his hairy leg, giving my best purring performance.

"I just knew he wouldn't jerk away from me, curse or fling a rock at me. No, as I knew he would, he picked me up and murmured, "Hey, kitty."

"From that moment on, my Pet Man and I were totally bonded and, with some insistence from the grandkids, I was taken home with them and installed as Miss Queen Kitty, ruler of the entire domicile and all its inhabitants within.

"I was immediately taken to the vet and spayed and given all my shots, just like I'd been born in the household.

"I was a Happenin' Kitty. I now had a nice home with lots of soft furniture, beds and rugs. I was given a real nice backyard to hunt in with a high rock wall observation perch, lots of big oak trees to climb, birds to hunt – more about that anon – squirrels to fuss with and no other competing cats to contend with. Oh, yes, I'd landed in Cat Heaven, all right!

"I also acquired, in the bargain, a Pet Woman who didn't exactly cotton to me right away like my Pet Man did, but with only a little cute kitty behavior on my part, I have won her over. I did my soft, warm, furry, limp cat act for her only a few times before she, too, became mine!

"My Pet Man finally named me. I'm known now as "LC" for Lap Cat. Seems obvious to me.. That's what I am – a serious, dedicated lap cat. The second either of my Pet Humans makes a lap, you can bet I'll be there, nesting, arranging my boneless body for a comfortable nap. If one lap ceases to be, I merely ensconce myself in the other one.

"Oh, those laps! It's the most important reason to have a Pet Man and/or a Pet Woman. No, wait – it's the never empty food dish. No, it's the ever-present water glass on the nightstand by the bed, which I love to stick my face in to get a drink. Or, is it getting to watch, interestedly, the dishes being washed or the commode being flushed? Wow! Where does that water go?

"I really love running water – that's not a cat-thing, is it? Neither is licking my Pet Man's hand, but, what can I say? It tastes delicious.

"In my short life of maybe a year or so, I've truly never met a human I didn't like, and, if you come to visit my Pet Man and Woman, I'll prove it to you.

"I'll do some cute kitty stuff for you that you won't be able to resist. It tickles me to hear you silly humans say things like, "Ohhh, what a cute, widdle kitty you are, sweetheart, listen to you purr. I'll just pick you up and hold you. You're so soft and no claws either." Actually I haven't found much use for claws yet in my life.

"As long as My Pet Humans remain as well trained as they are, my life is good. No problems at all.

"My Pet Man has even softened toward my chasing an occasional bird around his back yard feeder. He does feel protective of his wild birds – they were, after all, here first. He knows, I think, it's my natural instinct as a hunter to stalk the unwary sparrow as I was forced to do as an abandoned orphan by the lake. But he also knows to keep me well fed as a protection for his birds. I'm not really serious about hunting, you know – I just sort of go through the motions.

"Oh, I see a lap being formed in there. Hey, let me in! I could use a nap and you need your lap warmed up!"

A Near-life Experience

Since I cannot rightfully claim to have experienced a "near-death" episode at any time in my rather long and convoluted existence, I deemed it appropriate at this juncture in the proceedings to recount the most recent of many personal adventures which I consider to be "near life."

I'm certain I do not exaggerate in calling such life-affirming occurrences "near-life."

If one has an activity which one enjoys doing "on Sunday for no pay" as I do, the chances for near-life experiences become much greater than they would if one's activities of work, or play for that matter, are not so interesting.

People have accused me of being too easy to please, if you can imagine. Isn't it a good thing to be easily satisfied?

I think so, even at the risk of criticism from those perfectionists who claim that "the satisfied man is lost," and that most civilized accomplishments in this world are initiated by people who are hard to please.

Well, that very well could be, and perhaps those strivers do enjoy their lives and would work on Sunday for no pay. But I can only speak for myself and my own definition of life and what I have to do before I can claim to be living or nearly living.

It is a simple thing. So simple it seems absurdly so. What

happens to assure me that life is really happening, I mean.

Some of you may be aware of what I do – besides invent "Different Stuff" every week, which itself I find to be a pleasurable activity, one which does indeed get done on Sunday for no pay. I paint pictures for a living, for a hobby, for a life-affirming occupation.

The simple, physical act of taking a gob of paint and smearing it on a canvas or piece of paper is what it's all about for this old geezer.

I discovered the joys of painting very early on in life and have never been sidetracked with such mundanities as legitimate employment. Even my stint in Uncle Sam's armed forces failed to deter me – I did portraits of my fellow soldiers (for money.) Which they sent home to their girl friends or mothers.

The act of painting – that is my near-life experience. And lucky, lucky me, it happens a lot. Sometimes not every time, lest you think the feeling of elevated existence will happen as I begin a small sketch somewhere in Big Bend, such as yesterday, or as I'm smearing a gob onto a canvas in my studio, such as next week, God willing, but it happens most times.

So the expression I've used to describe the life experiences I have had and do have, near-life, seems to be not entirely accurate.

Oh, well, it was just a play on words anyway and it sounded funny.

But, this is true – being so fortunate to be easy to please has meant that I've had many, many life-elevating experiences because of being of a simple turn of mind.

We are who we are, aren't we, not changing basically from birth? As my wise old Uncle Willie says, "Keep doin' what yer doin' and you'll keep gettin' what yer gettin'!"

Okay, I'll go with that. As long as I'm allowed.

Dr. Pill Improves Everything

Dr. Pill

The How-to-live-better Clinic and Shoe Repair is open, open, open!

Address: Wherever is Dr. Pill.

Hours: Whenever the world needs rescuing (24-7).

Fees: All fees and moneys collected buried in a coffee can in the backyard. (Fees, plural and moneys, plural, add up to a lot more than fee, singular, and money, singular.) Sorry, no Medicaid or checks.

This week's topic: The World's a Mess, Let's Make It Better!

The intrepid and indefatigable Dr. Pill, ever ready to step up to the plate in your hour of need – three men on, two out; three balls; two strikes; third down, seven yards for a first; love 40; one second left on the clock; two points down, let's go in a twisting, athletic move – a long three-point attempt from downtown and, oooh, ooh! Another catastrophe averted!

"Here are a few well-thought-out suggestions, suitable for afternoon TV broadcast when most audience members are nodding off for a little afternoon nap," says the good Dr. P. (He's only a psychologist you see, not a real doctor, so he must only use the title "Dr." not "D-o-c-t-o-r.")

"Suggestion No. 1: An old-fashioned, conservative (we think) idea would be to stop giving all that free hype to shallow, off-beat, gender disoriented entertainers and other minor celebrities who have written (via "ghost writers," probably) a book detailing the "hard times," "tough childhood" and "abuse" they have personally suffered – worse abuse, by the way, than YOU ever suffered. Never, never interview these weirdos on any form of public communication, radio, TV or newspaper. The world will be measurably improved by our not knowing.

"Suggestion No 2 for Making It Better:

Everyone should immediately stop trying to explain, justify or rationalize Martha Stewart.

"Suggestion No. 3: In the area of improving our daily lives, we should either gather up the world's entire production of cell phones, load 'em on barges, tow 'em out to the Marianas Trench in the Pacific Ocean (or Atlantic, whichever) and sink 'em without a trace or, and I say this compassionately, it should be required that habitual cell phone users, from nine years old to 90 years old, have the things permanently implanted on the sides of their heads and these implantees should receive a 12-volt shock if they ever stop blithering into their implants.

"Suggestion No. 4 and this one will really make things better! We will, with compassion, use a stun gun on anybody who tells us to "have a nice day" or attempts to give us a "high five" and we will double the power of our stun guns when anybody says "no problem" instead of "you're welcome" or "thank you."

"We will use real bullets, though, every time somebody injects the word "like" into an inappropriate space in a conversation, one bullet per "like." We should only "shoot to wound," however, in the still too common space filler "you know."

Last suggestion for this week: Dr. Pill is tired and needs a nap: "Use the new SUV "Hummer II" (the Pulverizer) as a garbage tamper at the city dump. This vehicle is wide enough, long enough and heavy enough to be an extremely efficient tamper of loose garbage. Just roll a Pulverizer up on top of a freshly dumped pile and, viola, your garbage is instantly compressed!

Note: the new Ford Perpetrator (formerly the Excursion) also fits the garbage compaction criteria.

Until next session, Dr. Pill says, "Got a problem? Duh!"

The search for the Inner self

Back, way back, in the olden times, the days of yore, before written language, before even spoken language, beyond unintelligible, guttural grunts passing between humanoid beings, there was only one being – one being per being, that is.

Nobody suspected there might be another person dwelling inside the outer person. It was enough, everybody thought, to have to deal with just the one organism inhabited by each individual entity.

But now, thanks to modern intellectualism and education, we should be aware that, strange as it may seem, there is within all of us a newly discovered "inner self."

Note that this "self," which supposedly resides somewhere in the dank depths of our psyches, is an invention of modern psychology to explain why we're all so miserable and inadequate.

Life was simple in the days of yore. One had but to bash an animal for food and drink from the creek. One didn't bother with conversation, meaningful relationships or providing for one's progeny.

You just bashed 'em a good one if they didn't behave. One good bash and a loud grunt or two took care of things.

Nobody ever felt inadequate or unfulfilled. Things went along swimmingly day-to-day with not a regret.

Now look at us! All worried about this inner self nonsense, paying big bucks to folks in nice suits to discuss our deficient lives, learning to wring our hands and wrinkle our foreheads with worry over the demands of the "child" within our wretched bodies.

(Then signing up for a Botox party to have our recently acquired worry lines removed.)

But wait! Your intrepid Different Stuff crack staff researcher has stripped his craggy physiognomy to the bone and discovered there is, indeed, an inner child and that child is a rotten, spoiled Brat!

He is conniving, deceptive and devious. He is demanding and malicious. He wants his way about everything all the time.

What an unredeemable monster is this inner child. He whines, wheedles, creates diversions, listens to reasons then ignores them and goes on to have his way.

He is an awful, horrible entity that you'd go out of your way to avoid if you could.

But, alas, you cannot. He is there. In residence. The apparently normal outer shell of our body is merely a transparent covering which barely hides this child of our inner, dank, dark regions.

You can easily see how much better off were those dim-bulb ancestors of ours – grunting, bashing, procreating, not regretting anything, not even knowing what an inadequacy was, not even realizing they may have been deficient or miserable.

They were simply too busy providing the necessities, bashing the kids and the little woman to even consider how bad off they were.

Whatever those other tribes over there in that god-forsaken desert were doing was of no concern to these ancestors of ours – they were over there and we were over here, everybody minding his own business.

They had nothing we wanted, for crying out loud.

But wait! Maybe our rotten, spoiled brat inner child might have somehow gotten the idea that those desert dwelling humanoids might actually have something he'd like to have.

So he decides he's going to go on over there and bash 'em a good one!

The Language of Art

"What is most real for me are the illusions I create with my paintings. Everything else is quicksand."
Eugéne Delacroix, 1827

Okay, having cited the quote uttered way back yonder by Mr. Delacroix, a very famous artist, we feel there is no need to put it into other words at all. It is so self-explanatory. But we do feel compelled to explain how to explain Art.

Our crack staff of assistant writers has compiled a list of definitions which will no doubt be helpful the next tine you get into a discussion with an artist.

They call it "The Different Stuff Glossary of Art Terms." What follows is a partial list from the full compendium:

The Glossary of Art Terms "or stuff you need to know to either do or talk about art."

1. Brush – a hairy stick.
2. Paint – the gooey stuff that's all over the hairy stick.
3. Palette – the artist's friend who is a girl.
4. Easel – adverb meaing not difficult, as "heck, that's easel to do!"
5. Abstract – to get in the way of, as "please do not abstract my view."

6. Canvas – cloth upon which the artist daubs the gooey stuff that's on the hairy stick.

7. Painty – describing the surface of the canvas that has lots of paint on it.

8. Painterly – same as number 7, only with one more syllable.

9. Goosh – the noise made by paint being squeezed from a toob.

10. Toob – the thing that holds the gooey stuff.

11. Par – a mark on the studio wall that indicates how high up the painting should be.

12. Irving – a painting which is not quite up to par.

13. Art – first name of a man who once bought an Irving.

14. Turpentine or "turps" – what artists drink with their bacon and eggs.

15. Coffee – a liquid used to thin paint. (Beer works as well).

16. Steak – what the artist ate after Art bought the Irving.

The reader should bear in mind while discussing art with the artist that artists are an extremely sensitive lot and need to handled with extraordinary care and concern. They have a tendency to throw tantrums over negative reviews of their work.

When you go to a museum or gallery to look at art, you must also keep in mind how important it is that you look serious and "arty."

How do you do that, you may well ask. Here's how.

1. When you stop in front of a painting, assume the "parade rest" position, as in the military with both feet firmly planted about a foot apart, hands clasped behind your back, studious look on your face, slightly frowning, assimilating information about the work, somewhat quizzical expression invading your features as you try to remember several of the cogent definitions from the Glossary.

2. Dress funny.

This 'n' That Stuff

Yes, it's time once again for some spring cleaning. Here in the Different Stuff Corporate World Headquarters, we have amassed a huge quantity of bits of paper of all kinds – lined, unlined, torn, neatly scissored, large pieces, tiny scraps – with scribblings of ideas, notes of profundities, which passed through our mind at warp speed, along with myriad stuff we wrote down only because we were amused by how it looked or sounded.

We spindle, fold and mutilate these bits of wisdom and bon mots until the file which is round veritably runneth over, then we clean it out, save whatever appeals to us at the moment and add the rest to the landfill.

We will herein, with, of course, the use of our ubiquitous, never-ending supply of black dots, list for our own if for no one else's amusement and edification, the crème de la crème from our leftover pile of round file-isms.

We are perpetually amused, perhaps too easily so, by unusual words we hear – and sometimes make up – such as:

· WIERPED – a combination of "weird" and "warped." Not a real word – yet.

· PERSPICACIOUS – having or showing great insight. A real word and a favorite of mine, along with:

· VACUOUS – empty-head, inane.

Feel free, dear reader, to employ these words in your daily

conversations, as well as any of the following combinations of words or thoughts which you might find useful.

I, myself, regard much of verbal detritus as superfluous and nonsensical, good for naught but an occasion of lightheartedness – not a bad thing.

· This from some philosopher or another. "Man is certainly stark mad; he can't make a flea, yet he makes gods by the dozens."

· From old Uncle Willie, ever ready with the profunditry: "Ya cain't get lard less'n ya boil the hog!"

We think there is no dearth of useable wisdom in both of these emanations.

A truism now from the ever-present Mr. Anonymous:

· "Victory belongs to he who makes the second-to-last mistake." This is certainly true in basketball.

· Still waters run deep, as we've heard our entire lives, but still waters also become stagnant.

Oh, there are a million of 'em overflowing the spindle and the file that is round:

· To those of us who seek individuality, "fashion" is just a word. That one, I'm fairly certain, was uttered first by your correspondent.

· "Time is of no importance to those who seek excellence." I can't give credit as to who first said that. I don't know. But I do use it quite a bit in answer to the insipid question, "How long did it take you to paint that?" My other answer is "about 50 years and four hours."

Let me say now, as I wind down this week's epistle and put away my Pentel Rolling Writer 'til next time, I sincerely hope I have not caused any of you to experience, as you've read from my Round File Stiff, that sinking sensation like you were slowly settling to the bottom of the ocean, or to put it in one word:

· ENNUI – a feeling of mental weariness from lack of interest; boredom, in other words.

· BOREDOM – one of the most destructive mental conditions known to man.

To order additional copies of
Different Stuff

Name _____

Address _____

_____

$15.95 x _____ copies = _____

Sales Tax   _____
(Texas residents add 8.25% sales tax)

Please add $3.50 postage and handling   ___ _____

Total amount due: _____

Please send check or money order for books to:

WordWright.biz, Inc.
P.O. Box 1785
Georgetown, TX 78627

For a complete catalog of books,
visit our site at
http://www.WordWright.biz

Printed in the United States
1336500004B/187-207